Bed, Breakfast, and Murder

Jenna St. James

Jenna St. James Books

Ryli Sinclair Mystery Series (cozy)

Picture Perfect Murder
Girls' Night Out Murder
Old-Fashioned Murder
Bed, Breakfast & Murder
Veiled in Murder
Bachelorettes and Bodies
Rings, Veils, and Murder
Next Stop Murder
Gold, Frankincense & a Merry Murder
Heartache, Hustle, & Homicide

Sullivan Sisters Mystery Series (cozy)

Murder on the Vine
Burning Hot Murder
PrePEAR to Die
Tea Leaves, Jealousy, & Murder

Copper Cove Mystery Series (cozy)

Seaside & Homicide

A Witch in Time Series (paranormal)

Time After Time
Runaway Bride Time (novella)

A Trinity Falls Series (romantic comedy)

Blazing Trouble
Cougar Trouble

DEDICATION

I want to dedicate this book to M. Take it from me, there is nothing more therapeutic than writing. Take all the different emotions you are experiencing right now as you travel this journey…and kill "him" off.

To Lauren Dottin-Radel…although we have never met face-to-face, your encouragement touches my heart. I hope I gave you a little of what you asked for.

As always, to my mom and sister for their unending support and love.

And to James, thanks for pushing me when I want to throw in the towel and cry. And by pushing, I mean reminding me that you want to travel when you retire, and I better start putting my fingers and brain to work because crying isn't going to get you a trip to the islands! LOL.

CHAPTER 1

"That's quite the getup you got there, Aunt Shirley."

I sat down on my great-aunt's bed and stared in horror at the outfit she was holding up in front of the mirror. Bright floral print, elastic scoop neck dress, with three ruffled tiers ending at her knees. Around the top tier and armholes little multi-colored tassels were sewn into the dress.

"You like?" Aunt Shirley twirled, causing the tassels to airlift.

It was absolutely hideous.

The only saving grace was that it sort of matched the newly-dyed purple hair she was currently sporting. A couple months ago, my Aunt Shirley had shaved one side of her head. Now that it had grown out, she had these wispy tuffs of hair sticking out the left side of her head. Today the tuffs were purple. Tomorrow, who knows.

My Aunt Shirley was a true old maid. She'd never married nor had kids. Instead, she ran away to Los Angeles when she was in her early twenties and became a private investigator. Throughout the nineteen sixties and seventies, my aunt was a true Charlie's Angels type chick before it was even popular. Of course, to hear her tell, the series was based loosely on her life.

Now she lived at Oak Grove Manor, an assisted living facility in Granville, Missouri. She also helps out at the *Granville Gazette,* the newspaper where I also work. Aunt Shirley has no background in anything other than stakeouts and telling whoppers about how she used to sleep with all the hottest Hollywood men back in the day. But my boss, Hank Perkins, loved having her around the office.

Because I didn't want to hurt her feelings, and we needed to go soon, I decided to go with a lie on the dress. "Love it. Is it new?"

"Sure is," Aunt Shirley preened. "It's just one of the birthday dresses I bought for myself. The brochure for our murder mystery weekend said we'd have dinner and cocktails our first night. So I want to look extra snazzy in case I need to catch the eye of a hunky dude."

I suppressed a groan. "I thought you and Old Man Jenkins were an item?"

Aunt Shirley cackled. "He's my assisted-living beau. I get outside this place, and I'm fair game for anyone who thinks they can tame me!"

God help us all.

"How much more do you have to pack?" I asked. "We want to be on the road this morning by eleven so we can miss all the Friday evening traffic."

"Don't get your knickers in a twist. I'm almost done."

I looked at her makeup bag, which was actually bigger than her suitcase. "There are three other people riding in the Falcon. And we're only going to be gone for two days. You don't need to pack your whole closet."

Aunt Shirley closed the lid to the suitcase and snorted. "First off, the Falcon's trunk is large enough to hold three dead bodies.

She'll be able to hold a couple suitcases no problem. Secondly, I'm a lady, and a lady can never have too many outfits."

I rolled my eyes, but wisely kept my mouth shut. The Falcon Aunt Shirley was referring to was her pride and joy. A 1965 turquoise Ford Falcon with purple flames on the sides. Under the hood was a stock 302 with an Edelbrock fuel injection. The barely-there dashboard was done in the same turquoise color, and the bucket seats in the front and bench seat in the back were pristine white with turquoise stitching.

And now the Falcon is *my* pride and joy.

I helped Aunt Shirley wheel her luggage out into the deserted hallway and down to the elevator. "Have you spoken much to your new neighbors across the hall?"

Aunt Shirley glared at me. "No. Why would I? You remember what happened to the last ones, right? Besides, I can already tell I don't like these ones. There's something shifty about them."

Again I wisely kept my mouth shut.

Old Man Jenkins was waiting for us in the lobby. He was a good foot shorter than Aunt Shirley, around ninety years old, bald, and looked as though a strong wind would knock him down. But he was gaga for Aunt Shirley.

I loaded the suitcases in the back of the Falcon while the two love birds said goodbye to each other. Once Aunt Shirley was in, we waved farewell to Old Man Jenkins, and took off for the newspaper office to check in one last time.

Hank was still a little put out that Aunt Shirley and I were leaving for the weekend, but seeing as how I was pretty much his star reporter, he only gave me a little grief.

My boss, Hank Perkins, was a retired Marine who still walks the walk and talks the talk. Once a Marine, always a Marine. Oorah! There are two loves in his life—his wife and his newspaper. In that order.

Mindy was definitely the angel and anchor in the relationship. She was as gentle and kind as he was mean and surly. She had platinum blonde hair that was teased for miles, wore skin-tight Capri pants, neon colored off-the-shoulder shirts or sweaters, and designer high-heeled shoes. She's also got more herbal tea choices on hand than Carter's got liver pills. I just recently learned the etymology behind that saying. It wasn't at all what I thought it was. So now I'm using the phrase whenever I can.

Aunt Shirley and I sauntered into the newspaper office around ten. This was our last stop before we loaded up at Mom's to leave for the trip. I had to admit, I was giddy with excitement.

When Aunt Shirley first announced she wanted to do a murder mystery weekend, I was totally against it. Aunt Shirley and I seem to find enough trouble on our own—three different murders in about five months. Not a very good track record for anyone keeping track. But she lured me in with the promise of some wine tasting.

"I see by the way you're moseying in here so late that you both are still going on this ridiculous excursion," Hank snarled around his signature unlit cigar.

"Now Hank," Mindy soothed, "leave the girls be. They deserve this vacation. This is the first time they've taken off since the unfortunate incident in February."

The "unfortunate incident" Mindy's referring to was the near-death experience Aunt Shirley and I almost suffered at the hands of Aunt Shirley's crazy neighbors.

"I don't suppose there's any chance you two will stumble across a murder or two, is there?" Hank asked. "Usually you two are good for that."

I narrowed my eyes at Hank. "The only dead bodies we'll see this weekend will be the ones that are in the script. That I can promise you."

"Yep," Aunt Shirley agreed. "This is our weekend to relax and not worry about people trying to kill us for a change. Just a couple girls drinking wine and watching men."

I rolled my eyes at Mindy. "The drinking wine, yes. The watching men, no." I turned to Aunt Shirley. "You are the only one that's single on this trip."

"Oh, no! What about Old Man Jenkins?" Mindy asked. "Are you two not seeing each other anymore?"

Aunt Shirley opened her mouth to answer, but I cut her off. "Don't ask about that weird relationship. Her response won't make any sense. Anyway, we just came in to say goodbye and let you know, Hank, that I'll write up something while I'm down there for an entertainment and travel piece for the paper."

Hank yanked the unlit cigar out of his mouth. "I'd rather have an article on a nice murder, but I guess your namby-pamby fluff article will have to do."

I physically bit my lip to keep from sticking my tongue out at him. "Mindy, I'll miss you. Hank…well, I'll see you when I see you."

Hank grinned at me. "You be careful down there, kid."

"What about me," Aunt Shirley pouted.

Hank chuckled. "The day I have to tell you to watch your back will be the day you go to a permanent nursing home."

"True dat!" Aunt Shirley cackled as we walked out the door.

It takes less than five minutes to drive to my mom's house from the newspaper building. Of course, it takes less than five minutes to drive pretty much anywhere in this town because Granville had a population of just over ten thousand.

Mom's house was a large, two-story Victorian with a wooden wrap-around front porch. My favorite part of Mom's house—outside of the newly remodeled kitchen and bathroom—was her library. All four walls were filled with recessed bookshelves holding hundreds of books. Along with the gas fireplace, she'd also added a large dome-shaped skylight for just the right ambiance.

I was glad to see Garrett's police-issued vehicle in the driveway. My brother, Matt, had recently graduated from the police academy and now worked as a policeman for the Granville Police Department.

"Looks like everyone's here," I mused.

Aunt Shirley clapped her hands in glee. "Let's go solve us a murder!"

***

"You sure you've got everything?" Garrett's lips brushed against my ear, sending shivers down my spine.

I hid my smile so he wouldn't gloat at my obvious delight. "This is the last of it." I shove Mom's suitcase to the side and Garrett reached up and closed the Falcon's trunk.

Garrett Kimble was ten years older than me, with jet-black hair styled short from his military days, and the bluest eyes I'd ever seen. After leaving active duty, he worked for the Kansas City Police Department until my brother, Matt, talked him into applying for the job opening in Granville. He and Matt met at a veterans convention.

"So who lost the Rock, Paper, Scissors war?" Garrett teased.

"Me." I stuck out my lower lip in what I hoped was an adorable pout so he'd feel sorry for me. "I have to bunk with Aunt Shirley for the weekend. Mom and Paige have the other room."

I could tell by his twitching lips that he was trying to hide his smile. "Well, then promise me you and your aunt will stay out of trouble."

I kissed him quickly on the mouth. "I can definitely promise you I'm going to do nothing but wine taste and…well, wine taste!"

Aunt Shirley was already in the front seat, bouncing up and down like a kid in a toy store. Mom and Doc Powell were saying goodbye on the porch, and Matt and Paige were snuggled up by the backseat door, mooning over each other.

Even though neither one had said anything, I knew the last couple months had been stressful for Matt and Paige. They were really wanting a baby, but so far they weren't successful. The added pressure of Aunt Shirley constantly making reference to the lack of bouncing a baby on her knee wasn't helping.

Aunt Shirley stuck her head out the window. "Let's go! We ain't got all day."

I sighed and kissed Garrett one last time. "Miss me?"

He held my head in his hands and brushed his thumb across my right cheek. "Always, Sin." He laid his forehead against mine. "Remember…try not to get into any trouble this weekend."

CHAPTER 2

"It's absolutely beautiful," Mom said as we drove under the wrought iron archway welcoming us to Mystery Farms.

"Breathtaking," Paige agreed.

The long, paved driveway that led to the bed and breakfast was lined on each side with enormous oak trees. About fifty yards from the house was a large horse stable. According to the brochure, Mystery Farms had six horses for use. I couldn't wait to go horseback riding.

I pulled up in front of the main house and parked in the circle drive. Paige was right…the pale yellow, two-story farmhouse with white shutters and large white pillars attached to the wraparound porch was breathtaking. Rocking chairs and benches sat on the wide-planked wood front porch. Hanging flower baskets and colored flower pots were also scattered around the porch. It was perfect. Add the Missouri backdrop of gently rolling green hills, and I couldn't wait to spend the weekend relaxing here.

The front door opened and a middle-aged couple walked down the steps hand-in-hand to greet us.

"Welcome to Mystery Farms Bed and Breakfast," the man said. "My name is Gary Wainwright, and this is my wife, Cybil."

Gary Wainwright towered over his wife by a foot or two. He was fit and trim, with short black hair and warm brown eyes. I liked him immediately.

Cybil Wainwright looked like she packed a pretty powerful punch in a little body. I was willing to bet she spent a lot of time outdoors helping with the horses. Her wavy, chin-length hair and genuine smile helped to soften her angular features.

"Your place is just gorgeous." Mom shook Cybil's hand then turned to the rest of us. "This is my daughter, Ryli, and my daughter-in-law, Paige." We each took turns shaking hands. "And this is Aunt Shirley."

The Wainwrights' eyes were as big as saucers as they took in Aunt Shirley's hair. It was kind of humorous the way her purple, grown-out fluff was blowing in the slight breeze.

"Can I help you carry in your bags, Aunt Shirley?" Gary asked.

"Nope," Aunt Shirley said. "I got it. Keeps me young."

"Well then," Cybil said, "follow me, and I'll show you where you check in."

We gathered our luggage and followed her up the stairs and into the farmhouse. I gasped as I took in my surroundings. The inside was just as spectacular as the outside.

The wide, curved staircase was definitely the focal point of the foyer. It also didn't hurt that the foyer was twice the size of my bedroom back in Granville. Dark, hardwood floors went on as far as I could see. The wool, hand-woven floor rugs and lace doilies were a perfect country contrast.

"This is my niece, Dayna Bowers," Cybil said as she led us farther into the room.

Dayna was probably in her mid-twenties, with brown hair and hazel eyes. She was pretty and petite and had the same physical features as her aunt.

"She will get you guys checked in," Cybil continued. "Dayna also helps out in the kitchen and with housekeeping. So if you need anything, she's your girl. I better get back outside to greet our next guests."

"Welcome to Mystery Farms," Dayna said as her aunt walked out the front door. She motioned us over to the large, check in counter she was standing behind. "I have Janine and Paige in the Parker Pyne room, and Shirley and Ryli in the Miss Marple room."

Aunt Shirley laughed. "First off, you can call me Aunt Shirley, everyone does. And secondly, are all the rooms named after characters from Agatha Christie novels?"

Dayna smiled. "Yes, ma'am. We also have the Hercule Poirot and Harley Quin rooms."

"What about Tommy and Tuppence's room?" Aunt Shirley asked.

Dayna laughed. "The Beresford room belongs to Uncle Gary and Aunt Cybil, of course!"

We all stared in amazement at Aunt Shirley.

"What?" She threw her arms out wide and shrugged. "I do read you know. How do you think I got my sleuthing skills when I was a private investigator?"

Now why doesn't that surprise me?

Dayna opened a wooden box on the wall and withdrew two keys. She closed the door then handed Mom a key. "We do have an extra set of keys down here just in case you lose this one."

"Thank you," Mom said. "Hopefully that won't be necessary."

Dayna then handed me a key to our room. Mom gave Aunt Shirley a pointed look when Aunt Shirley made a grab for the key. "Why don't you let Ryli keep track of the key."

"Never," Aunt Shirley said as she successfully grabbed the key from Dayna.

Dayna smiled. "Just take the stairs to the top, turn left, and follow the hallway. That is the east wing. All guests stay in that wing. The room names are located on the doors. Dinner is served at five-thirty. Is there anything else I can do for you right now?"

"I don't believe so," Mom said.

"Are you sure you don't want me to help you with your suitcases?" I asked Aunt Shirley.

"The day I can't carry my own suitcase up a staircase is the day you need to take me out back and shoot me!"

I rolled my eyes at Paige. Pretty much everything with Aunt Shirley ended with us taking her out back and shooting her. One of these days I just might take her up on it.

Dayna laughed. "Okay. There's a library on the first floor here through those French doors and the hallway to the left. That will also take you to the back veranda which overlooks the pond and horse arena. Next to the library is Uncle Gary's private office. We ask that all guests limit themselves to the library and back veranda area. Now, go ahead and unpack, relax a little. I'll see you at five-thirty for dinner."

Cursing my bad luck on losing at Rock, Paper, Scissors, I followed everyone to the curved staircase. I paused and watched in amusement as Aunt Shirley tried to figure out how to carry not only her suitcase, but her even larger makeup bag up the stairs. There was no way.

"Here." She thrust the enormous makeup bag at me and slowly made her way up the stairs. I shook my head but didn't say anything as I struggled up the staircase carrying two massive suitcases.

Mom and Paige's room was first, so we dropped them off at the door. I told Mom we'd meet up with her and Paige in an hour and a half for dinner. After the long drive, I wanted to unpack and catch a quick cat nap.

Aunt Shirley pushed open the door to our room, and I followed her inside. One look and I knew I was in trouble—the bed.

The bed was a queen-sized, four-poster bed. That meant Aunt Shirley and I had to share a bed. The fact the bed sported a luxurious down comforter and feather pillows didn't console me much.

I still had to sleep with Aunt Shirley.

I also understood why they called it the Miss Marple room. There were lace doilies across the top of the large oak dresser, across the tops of the two lampshades, and under the TV. It was not my taste, but it was cute. I couldn't help but wonder what the Parker Pyne room looked like.

There were two windows in the room, which let in a lot of natural light. One window faced the front yard and the other window faced the horse stable. The view was perfect…even if the sleeping arrangements weren't.

I picked up a Mystery Farms brochure and read about the murder mystery weekend options. The Wainwrights had only been doing the packages for a year and a half. They featured three different murder mystery weekend packages. We were doing the

Not a Clue package. I had no clue what that even meant. Pun intended.

I walked across the room and opened the door to the bathroom. Instead of a shower, a porcelain white claw foot tub with pewter legs sat in the middle of the room. I could hear it calling my name. "I'm gonna take a bath real quick before dinner," I called out to Aunt Shirley who was still unpacking.

"Go downstairs and see if that nice girl, Dayna, has some antacids, would you?" Aunt Shirley demanded. "Your driving gave me heartburn, and I forgot to pack them."

I rolled my eyes and walked back into the bedroom area. "My driving didn't give you heartburn."

Aunt Shirley scowled at me. "It did, too. Now, go do an old woman a favor and get me some antacids."

I sighed at her typical Aunt Shirley passive-aggressive behavior but went to do what she asked. I've learned I have to pick and choose my battles with Aunt Shirley.

I was halfway down the curved staircase when I heard angry voices coming from the foyer. They were trying to whisper, but the more they tried to whisper, the more elevated they became.

"Why are you being like this?" Dayna demanded.

"You need to leave this alone," an angry male voice said.

"But I love you, Trent," Dayna insisted.

I heard a snickering grunt. "Honey, I'm not exactly a one-woman kinda man. You know what I mean? We have a good time and all, but don't go getting any ideas."

I heard sobbing and then a sniffle. "I'll tell my aunt and uncle what's been going on with us. They only let me see you because they never thought it would go as far as it has."

"Are you threatening me?" I didn't have to see this guy's face to realize he was livid. "You might want to think long and hard about that, Dayna. Nobody threatens me!"

I felt horrible for eavesdropping, but I didn't know what else to do. I knew if I went back upstairs empty-handed, Aunt Shirley would demand to know why I didn't have her antacids. Then I'd have to admit I overheard an argument, and before I knew it, I'd be knee-deep in something that wasn't any of my business.

I decided to take matters into my own hands and pretended to have a coughing fit as I went down the stairs. I figured that would give Dayna enough of a warning that someone was coming.

I have to admit, I was curious who she was arguing with. I also had to wonder if this was part of the whole murder mystery thing. But since they had no idea I would be coming down the stairs when I did, I didn't think it was part of the show.

This solving a fake murder could be more difficult than I first thought. I had no idea what was real and what was fake.

I reached the bottom of the stairs and saw Dayna take a step backward, distancing herself from an attractive-looking man. I could tell by her red face and the way she wouldn't look me in the eye she knew I had overheard.

The man looked to be in his early thirties, short blond hair, blue eyes, and a square, rugged jaw. And by the way his clothes molded to his athletic body, he definitely spent a lot of time outdoors.

"Oh. Hi, Ryli. This is Trent Starnes. He's in charge of the horses. I think you signed up to ride tomorrow didn't you? He's really good with horses. I'm sure you'll enjoy your time." Dayna seemed to ramble on and on. Now I really felt sorry for the poor girl.

Hoping to ease her discomfort, I turned to Trent and stuck out my hand. "It's nice to meet you, Trent."

Trent clasped my hand and then covered the top of my hand with his other hand, sandwiching me. "It's lovely to meet you, Ryli. Beautiful name for a beautiful woman." Trent flashed his straight, white teeth at me while he simultaneously rubbed his thumb over the top of my hand. I'm sure he thought it was charming, but I found it creepy and disgusting.

I tried to pull my hand back without drawing attention to myself, but I failed miserably. Aunt Shirley was right. It was time for me to start doing some serious weight lifting to get into better shape. When I was too puny to yank back my own hand, I was in big trouble.

My first impression of Trent Starnes was that he was a leech. What in the world did Dayna see in this jerk? He was good looking, yes. But that was about all he had going for him.

"Is there something I can get for you, Ryli?" Dayna asked.

I shifted my eyes from Trent to her. "Yes. Aunt Shirley has some heartburn and forgot to pack some antacids. I don't suppose you have any handy?"

"Of course." Dayna walked back behind the counter, bent down, and I could hear her rummaging around. I wanted to avoid eye contact with Trent, so I pretended to be interested in everything the room had to offer—everything but him.

After a few seconds Dayna stood up. "Here you go." She handed me the antacids and put the box back where it was. She still hadn't looked me in the eye, but I could tell she was trying not to cry.

I decided to hightail it out of there before things got anymore awkward. "Thanks. I guess I'll see you at dinner."

I looked over at Trent, which was a huge mistake. He gave me a lecherous grin and winked at me. Again, I'm sure he was going for charming, but I just found it revolting.

"Dinner will be a pleasure with you there, Ryli," Trent drawled out.

I ran up the stairs to get away from the two of them. Okay, that was a slight exaggeration. I walked briskly. There was no way I could physically run up a flight of stairs. Not even if someone was chasing me with a knife.

I stopped at the top of the stairs to see if I could hear them arguing again. I could, but I couldn't make out the words, just the tone. It didn't sound pretty.

I thought about whether or not I should mention what happened to Aunt Shirley. Mainly because I still wasn't sure if it was part of the murder mystery script or not. I decided to keep my mouth shut. No sense making a mountain out of a mole hill at this point.

I opened the door and was surprised to find the room empty. I was beginning to think Aunt Shirley gave up on me and went to see if Mom had any antacids, when I heard a splash from the bathroom. I walked over and knocked on the door.

"What?" Aunt Shirley hollered. "I'm trying to relax."

I gritted my teeth and counted to ten. A while back when I thought Aunt Shirley had been shot trying to save my life, I made a vow to turn over a new leaf. I was going to start having more patience with her. But the fact that she made me go downstairs and get medication she obviously didn't need just so she could take a bath—something she knew I wanted to do—well, let's just say I still had a long way to go when it came to patience and understanding with Aunt Shirley.

"I have your antacids," I snarled, not caring how mean I sounded.

"Just put them on the dresser," Aunt Shirley called out as though she didn't have a care in the world "I'll get them when I get out of the tub. This is a great tub. You're gonna love it!"

I shook my head and tossed the bottle onto the dresser. With the way things were going, I'd be the one chowing down on the antacids by the end of the night.

I wiped my damp forehead with the back of my hand and lifted both of the windows to let in a cool breeze. I then grabbed my suitcase and flung it on the bed and started to unpack. I'd just finished putting my undergarments in the drawer when I heard another vehicle approach the house. I glanced out the window and saw a newer model sedan pull into the circle drive and stop.

A young, beautiful redhead with long, wavy hair stepped out of the passenger side. She had on brown skinny jeans, a brown and jade tunic shirt, and designer high-heeled sandals that were wildly out of place. She was clutching a brown and pink purse that was almost twice her size.

"Stewart," the woman whined, "get off the phone! You've been on it since we left an hour ago."

The man—Stewart, I'm assuming—held up a finger and turned his back to her. I couldn't make out what he was saying, but by the hunch of his shoulders, I didn't think it was good news. He finally hung up and swung around to face the outraged woman. He ran his hands through his shaggy brown hair and scowled. "You know my business is important, Tina. Stop whining and get over yourself."

My mouth dropped. I wasn't used to men talking to women like that. Most of the men I knew, outside of Hank, were kind and respectful. But even Hank's demeanor wasn't outright rude. Hank was just Hank.

I heard a throat clear and figured the Wainwrights had stepped outside to greet their newest guest. Something told me that this weekend just got amped up to be explosive. I was about to turn around and finish unpacking when I saw a look lust cross Tina's face. Her mouth dropped open and her hand clutched her chest. She was gaping at the horse stable.

I knew better than to think that a horse made her have that look, so I walked over to the other window to see what was so appealing. I almost gagged. I should have known. Leaning in the stable doorway without a shirt on was Trent Starnes. I couldn't see his face from my vantage point, but something told me he had on that lecherous grin of his. Yep, this was definitely going to be an explosive weekend.

CHAPTER 3

"What on earth is that smell?" I asked as I walked out of the bathroom sneezing.

Not only did Aunt Shirley have on the hideous tasseled dress, but the most god-awful smell was coming from her.

"It's my new perfume. You like?"

I pinched my nose together and refrained from answering. "Did you put the whole bottle on?"

Aunt Shirley scowled at me. "It's expensive, so that means it's strong. That's how this kind of stuff works, you ninny."

Ummm…no.

"C'mon," I said. "It's five-fifteen and I'm hungry. Let's go meet our guests for the week and see a murder tonight."

Aunt Shirley clapped her hands together and ran over to get her huge, patent-leather pink purse.

"Why are you bringing that?" I asked. "It's dinner and we aren't leaving the house."

Aunt Shirley gave me a look of pure disgust. "Because there might be something in here we need when we discover our first body tonight!"

"Of course. What was I thinking?" I deadpanned. "Let's go get the others."

Mom and Paige were already in the hallway ready to go. We made our way down the staircase and followed the voices into the parlor. If the rest of the guests were anything like Stewart and Tina, this could be a very entertaining weekend.

The room was already packed by the time we shuffled in. I guess five-thirty dinner meant five-fifteen gab fest. Although, from the looks of the other guests, I wasn't sure I'd be mingling much outside of my immediate family.

Stewart was pressed into a corner, his back to us, talking on the phone. The guy really needed to give it a rest. Tina, dressed in a low cut, dark blue sheath dress, was leaning provocatively on the fireplace talking with Trent Starnes and drinking champagne. From the way his eyes kept creeping down her plunging neckline, he wasn't listening to a word she was saying.

A woman I hadn't met yet was shooting daggers at Trent and Tina. She was an attractive woman with short, blonde hair and a slim body. Unfortunately, she seemed to be suffering from severe allergies because her face was puffy and swollen.

Dayna came in carrying a tray of iced tea and champagne. She stopped so fast when she saw Trent and Tina, that I was afraid her tray was going to crash. I rushed over and helped to steady her.

"That's a lot of drinks to try and carry in one haul," I joked.

Fighting back tears, Dayna set the tray down and nodded. "There's champagne or iced tea here. Go ahead and take one. Dinner is almost ready." She rushed out of the room, not looking back.

I had a sudden urge to punch Trent Starnes in the face. I was saved from following through with that urge when Aunt Shirley, Mom, and Paige sidled up to me.

"That poor girl," Mom said. "Is everything okay?"

"No." I decided to go ahead and tell them about what I'd overheard in the foyer between Dayna and Trent when I came down to get Aunt Shirley some antacids.

Mom's brow furrowed. "Are you not feeling well, Aunt Shirley?"

Aunt Shirley grinned at me. "I feel fine. I just wanted some peace and quiet during my bath."

"I tried ours out, too," Paige said as she took a sip of her iced tea.

"Hello, guests!" Mr. and Mrs. Wainwright stepped into the parlor and walked hand-in-hand toward the center of the room. "Cybil and I want to welcome everyone to our murder mystery weekend here at Mystery Farms. We have a lot of familiar faces this time. I'm going to take a few minutes to introduce you all. So gather around, please."

We all made our way toward the center of the room where he and Cybil were standing. Everyone except Stewart—he was still in the corner on the phone.

"I'll start here," Gary Wainwright said, pointing to Paige. "This is Paige Sinclair. Next we have Janine Sinclair, Ryli Sinclair, and Aunt Shirley." Gary Wainwright turned to Aunt Shirley. "It's okay for everyone to call you Aunt Shirley, correct?"

"That's what I prefer."

"Okay. Aunt Shirley it is. The family is here celebrating Aunt Shirley's birthday all the way from Granville, Missouri.

Polite nods and murmurs greeted us.

Mr. Wainwright smiled and went on. "Over here we have Olivia Banner. She's from the Springfield area. Usually she brings her hubby along, but I see this time it's just you."

Olivia Banner gave a weak smile and blinked back tears. "Yes. Brian couldn't make it this time." I took a closer look at Olivia. At first I thought she had allergies, but now I realized her eyes were red and swollen from crying. From the way she twisted her wedding ring, I'd say there was trouble in paradise.

"And even though Mrs. Banner has been here before for this particular murder mystery, she promises not to give away any secrets!" Cybil added.

"That's right." Olivia gave us all a fake forced smile.

"Next is Stewart and Tina Collins from St. Louis." Gary Wainwright stopped talking and frowned. I guess it was the first time he'd noticed Stewart wasn't with the group.

"Stewart!" Tina Collins hissed. "Get off that phone and get over here!"

With his back still to us, Stewart lifted up a finger to signal one more minute. For the first time, I actually felt a little sorry for Tina.

"As I was saying," Mr. Wainwright continued, "Tina has been with us once before on a girls' weekend trip, but she hasn't seen this particular murder mystery. And this time she also brought her husband."

Why? He obviously doesn't want to be here.

"And last but not least, we have Colonel Musgaard," Gary Wainwright continued, obviously trying to ignore Stewart's disregard for everyone in the room. "The Colonel is visiting us from Hannibal."

Colonel Musgaard was a slightly overweight, middle-aged man with a salt and pepper receding hairline. He was dressed in a yellow t-shirt, tan blazer, and tweed pants. "Happy to be here, dear boy. Happy to be here."

We all followed the Wainwrights into the main dining room for dinner. The massive, cream colored dining room table sat ten people comfortably with two captain chairs on each end. A colorful Oriental rug sat under the table on the dark hardwood floor. A cream China hutch and matching buffet were pushed against the buttercream walls.

A plump woman with frizzy red hair was standing in the doorway that led to the kitchen. She stepped closer to the table once we all sat down. "Good evening. My name is Bessie Terrance, and I am your chef for the weekend. Tonight's meal will be a garden salad with all ingredients grown right here in our own garden. Peppercorn steak with baby potatoes, fresh-from-the-garden green beans, and homemade rolls with hand-churned butter. For dessert we have a lemon custard fruit tart."

Bessie had me at peppercorn steak. By the time she finished reciting the menu, my stomach was growling and my mouth was watering.

I was sandwiched between Tina Collins and foul-smelling Aunt Shirley with Mom, Paige, and Colonel Musgaard across from me. Poor Olivia Banner had to sit directly across from Stewart. I don't know if it was intentional or not, but separating Tina and Stewart seemed like a good move. Dayna and Trent each took a side and served us dinner and drinks as we all made small talk.

"Can I get you anything else?"

I turned to my left to tell Trent no thank you, when I realized he wasn't talking to me but to Tina. She giggled and took a long sip of her champagne. Without missing a beat, she reached out and caressed his leg as he stood near her chair. "Maybe later." She'd whispered low enough that only I overheard.

Stunned, I could do nothing but sit there stiffly. I knew my face had to be red from embarrassment…and anger. Never had I wanted to deck another human being as much as I wanted to deck Trent Starnes at this moment.

Dayna righted herself from having just poured Colonel Musgaard a drink. She caught my eye and I could tell she, too, had seen what had just transpired between Tina and Trent. I averted my eyes so I didn't further embarrass the poor girl.

The rest of the dinner and dessert passed without incident. Even though I hadn't done anything physical other than drive down to Mystery Farms, I could barely keep my eyes open. I wasn't sure what the rest of the night was going to bring or when the first murder would happen, but I was hoping it would happen soon before I keeled over.

"Let's take this party back into the parlor and have a nightcap before we all turn in," Gary Wainwright said at the end of dinner.

"I'm so full," Paige moaned. "I'm not sure I have room for a drink."

"I could probably have a little something-something," Aunt Shirley said.

Big surprise.

"In fact, a nice margarita would hit the spot after the lemon custard," Aunt Shirley continued.

"I'll see what I can do," Cybil Wainwright said. "I think Bessie has some fresh squeezed lemonade. How about that and tequila? Would that work for you?"

"You bet!" Aunt Shirley said.

We all made our way back into the parlor as Dayna and Trent served after-dinner drinks. Mom and Aunt Shirley were talking with Colonel Musgaard near the fireplace while Tina and Steward were hissing and spatting with each other in the corner. I sat down on the settee next to Olivia. She was staring intently at Trent while she nervously twisted her wedding ring.

"Can I join this party?" Paige asked with a smile.

I waited to see if Olivia would answer. When she didn't I motioned for Paige to sit down.

"Wasn't dinner amazing?" I asked as Paige sat down across from us in a wingback chair.

"It sure was," Paige agreed. "What was your favorite, Olivia?"

Olivia gave no indication she had heard Paige's question. Seems she was too busy throwing hate vibes Trent's way. I looked at Paige and shrugged my shoulders.

"Trent," Gary Wainwright called, "can you help Dayna pass out the champagne to everyone so we can toast Bessie on her wonderful meal and to a fabulous murder-filled weekend?"

Bessie, Cybil, and Dayna carried in trays filled with different drinks. "Go pull Mom away from that weird Colonel guy," I said. "I'll go snag us each a glass of champagne." I didn't wait for a response from Paige. I knew she never turned down champagne.

I walked over to where Dayna was carrying a tray of drinks. I smiled and told her how much I enjoyed everything so far. She tried to be polite, but her heart really wasn't into her response. Like Olivia, she couldn't take her eyes off Trent.

After grabbing two flutes, I walked over to where Mom, Aunt Shirley, and Paige were huddled. Colonel Musgaard had moved to sit alone in a chair by the fireplace.

Gary Wainwright lifted his flute in the air. "I always like to thank Bessie at the end of our first night together. She has been such an integral part of this business. Not only does she prepare the wonderful food we eat, but she also keeps our website up-to-date. You may not know it to look at her, but Bessie definitely knows her way around a computer. Please join me in raising a glass to Bessie."

"Here, here!" we all shouted.

I took a healthy gulp of my champagne and watched as Olivia sat down at the piano bench and began to softly play.

I looped my arm through Paige's and clinked my champagne glass with hers. I took another drink. "Hey, why aren't you drinking champagne? You love champagne."

Paige smiled. "I guess now's the perfect time to tell you. Matt and I found out last week I'm about seven weeks pregnant!"

CHAPTER 4

Mom, Aunt Shirley, and I erupted into screams. We each took turns hugging and congratulating Paige. I couldn't believe after all these months of trying we were gonna finally have a baby in the family.

"I wanted to wait for the perfect time to tell you guys," Paige said. "I'm just sorry I won't be able to do any wine tasting on Sunday."

"This is the best news," Mom said as she wiped a tear off her cheek.

"When are you due?" I asked.

Paige looked adoringly at Mom. "November 22. We counted back, and that means I got pregnant right around Valentine's Day. Guess those chocolates of yours worked."

"And Mindy's negligee," I reminded her. I'd gotten the same gift.

"How did Matt take the news?" Mom asked.

Paige laughed. "Shocked. Excited. Scared. Just like me."

Aunt Shirley patted Paige's arm. "You both will be great parents."

I was shocked at Aunt Shirley's sincerity. I mean, I knew she wanted a baby to bounce, I just thought it was for purely selfish reasons.

Aunt Shirley scowled at me. "Stop looking at me like that. I can be nice when I want to be."

I opened my mouth for a snappy comeback, but was interrupted by a squeal from across the room. Tina Collins was standing next to Colonel Musgaard's chair, her hands over her mouth.

"Looks like we got our first murder," Aunt Shirley said gleefully. She took off for Colonel Musgaard's body, the tassels on her dress flying in all directions.

Aunt Shirley stopped in front of Colonel Musgaard and then bent down to peer in his face. The Colonel's eyes were shut and the drink in his hand was dangerously close to spilling.

Aunt Shirley sniffed at the drink then sniffed at Colonel Musgaard's face again. At the same time Colonel Musgaard let out a loud sneeze…right in Aunt Shirley's face.

"Good God, woman. You have enough perfume on to kill someone!" Musgaard exclaimed before he closed his eyes once more and pretended to be dead.

I couldn't help it…I exploded into giggles.

"Who served him the drink?" Aunt Shirley demanded, obviously choosing to ignore Colonel Musgaard's declaration.

Dayna looked at Trent Starnes and Cybil Wainwright before shrugging. "I'm not sure. We all were carrying a mixture of drinks on our trays."

"Who made up the drinks?" Tina asked, getting into the spirit of the game.

I thought that was a great question.

Again Dayna shrugged. "I don't know. They were already poured and sitting on the trays when I got to the kitchen."

I turned to Bessie. "Did you pour them?"

Bessie shook her head, and red frizz went flying. "I didn't. I noticed they were already poured the last time I went back into the kitchen."

I looked at Gary Wainwright to gauge his reaction. He looked just as confused as the other suspects. These people were great actors.

"I called the police," Cybil Wainwright announced.

A few seconds later there was a knock at the front door. I barely suppressed a giggle. That was the fastest call time I'd ever experienced. And I've had Garrett on the end of a phone line before, telling him I'd found a dead body. Garrett's call time was still a little longer than this.

Gary and Cybil left the room to get the door, and I went to go stand by Aunt Shirley. Olivia was still softly playing the piano. I guess since she'd already participated in the murder mystery before, she didn't want to risk dropping a hint. Stewart was busy looking at his watch, obviously bored.

"Ladies and gentlemen, may I have your attention?" Gary and Cybil returned with a distinguished-looking man in his late seventies or early eighties. His face was weathered from years in the sun. He was tall and fit—he looked like he could fight his way out of any given situation. His dusty cowboy boots made a heavy thud sound as he walked on the hardwood floor. "May I introduce Lester Simpson, our Sheriff."

Sheriff Simpson tipped his cowboy hat in greeting and slowly made his way over to where we were gathered around Colonel Musgaard. He stopped short when he saw Aunt Shirley. He carefully took in her funky hair and tasseled dress.

Sheriff Simpson winked at Aunt Shirley. "Well, ma'am, aren't you a lovely vision tonight."

Aunt Shirley tittered, and her face turned pink. "Why, Sheriff, thank you so much!"

I'll never understand the charismatic charm my Aunt Shirley has over men. I'm not sure if it's the outlandishness they are attracted to or what exactly makes men fall over themselves to please her.

"So this must be the dead guy?" Sheriff Simpson leaned down and peered into Colonel Musgaard's face. He looked pointedly at the glass in Colonel Musgaard's hand, then placed his own hand against the side of Colonel Musgaard's neck. "Yep. He's a goner. I think his drink was poisoned."

Again, I barely suppressed a giggle. I'd stumbled across my fair share of dead bodies over the last few months, and none of them were this simple. Usually it ended with me screaming, crying, and even throwing up on occasion. This was definitely the best way to discover a dead body. And the simple fact that the Sheriff could deduce Colonel Musgaard had been poisoned simply because he saw a glass was even better.

"I will need to question each of you as to where you were right before the body was discovered and possible motives. I'll start with the Wainwrights and work my way down the list to employees and then guests. Since it's late, I probably won't get to guests until tomorrow morning."

Thank God. I need a bath, hot tea, and a warm bed.

"You know, Sheriff," Aunt Shirley said. "My niece, Ryli, and I have had our fair share of run-ins with poisoning. Ryli here was given Ketamine against her will, and recently we were both drugged with Ambien and other sleeping pills."

Sheriff Simpson's eyes widened in shock. "Is that so?"

Aunt Shirley nodded. "And I used to be a licensed private investigator years ago in Los Angeles. We could probably be very helpful to you in your investigation."

Sheriff Simpson smiled. "Then I look forward to talking with you tomorrow."

"It's a date," Aunt Shirley said. "Now, if you don't mind, it's late and my dentures need to come out."

With that Aunt Shirley turned and walked out of the parlor. Mom, Paige, and I followed close behind. We had just gotten to the bottom of the stairs when Aunt Shirley turned around.

"I get it!" She was laughing so hard she had to bend over to catch her breath. "Colonel Musgaard in the parlor with poison! That's clever!"

"Hey," Paige said, "that *is* funny. I didn't even get it until now. That's why he was wearing that ugly yellow t-shirt under the tan blazer."

Gary Wainwright had moved to the archway between the parlor and foyer. He caught my eye and gave me a sly smile and a nod.

Aunt Shirley was right…this WhoDunIt birthday weekend was definitely going to be a good time. No forever murder, no blood, no hostage negotiation with a crazy killer. Just clean, fun murder.

We said good night to Paige and Mom, congratulating Paige one more time on her pregnancy before retiring to our bedrooms.

"That's pretty cool about the baby, huh?" I asked as I retrieved my pajamas from the dresser.

Aunt Shirley sat down on the edge of the bed and sighed. "It sure is. It'll be nice to have a baby running around."

I stopped getting undressed and stared at her. "Do you ever regret not having children?"

Aunt Shirley gave me a sad smile. "No. It was my choice to make, and I feel I made the right one. But it will be nice to be around something so young and new."

"Am I getting too old for you to hang around?" I joked, hoping to pick up her mood.

Aunt Shirley snickered. "Just a little bit. Now go take your bath and leave me alone. I need my beauty sleep so I look hot tomorrow for my date with the Sheriff!"

I shook my head at the fact that only Aunt Shirley would think talking with a Sheriff about a murder could be construed as a date. Most people would be up half the night sick with worry. Only Aunt Shirley would be up half the night planning her wardrobe.

I went into the bathroom and ran my bath water. I dropped in Vanilla Lavender bath salts and went back to ask Aunt Shirley a question while the tub filled.

"Aunt Shirley, do you think the tension between Dayna and Trent is for real or part of the murder mystery drama?"

Aunt Shirley shut off her lamp and snuggled down deep on her side of the bed. "I've noticed that, too. I don't know. I think it's real. Kinda hard to fake that kind of raw emotion."

I nodded. "I think so, too. Shame he wasn't the one killed tonight."

Aunt Shirley chuckled. "There's always tomorrow."

CHAPTER 5

"So are you having fun?" Garrett asked.

I shifted my phone from my right ear to my left ear. "Yes. I'm actually surprised at how fun this is. Great food, and we already had our first murder last night. The best part was when the guy who is supposed to be dead *sneezed* because Aunt Shirley had on too much perfume and she was leaning over him examining him! It was so funny. Oh, and Aunt Shirley has a date today with the guy that plays the Sheriff. So she's having a great birthday weekend."

"Sounds like a good time." Huge pause. "Anything else new?"

I growled. "Garrett Kimble, did you already know about the baby?"

Garrett laughed. "Only last night. Matt, Nick, Officer Ryan, and I got together out at my house and Matt made the announcement. He figured Paige was going to say something last night, so it was okay to tell us."

I gave a little squeal. "I'm super excited for them. A baby!"

"Yeah," Garrett sighed.

I heard the wistfulness and started to panic. Even though Garrett hadn't started pressuring me into a stronger commitment, I knew the time was coming. He would be thirty-nine this year, and he was ready to settle down and have a family. I knew it, but it didn't help with the anxiety I always started to feel. It's not that

I'm not ready to settle down, it's more I'm not sure if I'll be any good at it. I still sniff my clothes to see if they are clean. I barely remember to feed my cat. I don't cook very well, and I worry about what kind of wife and mother I will be.

"Well, I need to head over to the office soon," Garrett said. "Thanks for calling, Sin. Have fun finding another dead body today."

I laughed. "I bet you never thought you'd hear yourself say those words to me, did you?"

Garrett joined in the laughter. "You got that right. Usually I'm lecturing you on *not* finding dead bodies."

I hung up, threw the phone down on the bed, and listened to Aunt Shirley getting ready in the bathroom. We still had another twenty minutes before breakfast was served at eight.

I reached over to shut the bedroom window when I heard arguing out by the barn. I peered down closer through the screen and saw Trent Starnes and Olivia Banner going at each other. I couldn't hear what was being said, but Trent was doing a lot of shrugging and shaking his head. In a flash, Olivia reached out and slapped Trent across the face.

But why were they fighting? Was this part of the act, too? Or were Trent and Olivia somehow entangled with each other? That could account for the hostility, puffy eyes, and wedding ring twisting she'd been doing last night.

"What're you looking at?" Aunt Shirley asked.

I let out a little scream and turned. "What the—you scared me to death!" I laid my hand over my heart and prayed it wouldn't leap out of my chest.

"You big sissy," Aunt Shirley said. "When're you gonna toughen up?"

"I was going to wish you a happy birthday today, but I think I'll change my mind if you keep it up. So how old are you this year?"

Aunt Shirley snorted. "I'll never tell." She'd let it drop that this year was an important one, so I was going with seventy-five.

Aunt Shirley put up her fists and took up a fighting stance. "Wanna try and give me birthday swats? I kinda feel like kicking your butt this morning."

I ignored her and turned back to the window hoping to see some more of the fight going on outside. Unfortunately, Trent was closing the door to the barn and Olivia was running back to the house.

"Olivia Banner and Trent Starnes were outside fighting. I couldn't hear what was being said, but Olivia slapped Trent across the face."

Aunt Shirley whistled and crept toward the window. "Sorry I missed that little drama."

I chuckled. "It was pretty entertaining. Let's go down and see if anyone is having coffee or something in the parlor."

I turned from the window and really took in Aunt Shirley's outfit for the day. She was dressed in what can only be described as a floral pantsuit romper. Her love affair with floral patterns was tragic.

"Is that a one-piece pantsuit?" I asked.

"Yep." She turned around so I could see the zipper in the back. "I just step into it and zip it up. It even has pockets." Aunt Shirley stuck her hands in the pockets and pulled the pockets out from the pantsuit, causing the pantsuit legs to billow out like a clown outfit.

"It's quite…something."

I had no idea how to compliment the hideous outfit. It was almost as bad as the tassel dress she'd worn last night. I had to wonder where she was buying her clothes lately. Her wardrobe had suddenly taken on a more dramatic flair.

"Luckily this outfit came in the mail a few days ago, just in time for the trip. I want to impress the Sheriff today with my riding skills, but still look feminine. I can't straddle a horse in a skirt. That would be tacky."

"So right on that," I deadpanned as I grabbed my phone off the bed and headed downstairs to the parlor. I was on a mission to find Mom and Paige…and caffeine. It was too early to tangle with Aunt Shirley without my caffeine.

A gentleman I hadn't met yet was seated in front of the fireplace sipping coffee. He was thin and had thick dark hair. He was dressed in a suit and tie with a matching silk handkerchief in his breast pocket. I placed him around Mom's age…mid-fifties. He looked up and smiled when Aunt Shirley and I entered the room.

"I can't wait to see what the day brings," Tina Collins chirped gaily as she and Stewart sailed into the parlor. She had on a pair of jeans so tight they looked painted on and a low-cut, hunter green sweater. Very low cut.

"Those pants are so tight I can see her religion!" Aunt Shirley joked. Unfortunately, her voice carried and Tina heard her.

"What did you say?" Tina demanded.

Aunt Shirley hooted. "I said you might want to yank that sweater up…we can see clear to the Promised Land!"

I nudged Aunt Shirley and gave her a warning look. While funny, it wasn't appropriate. Especially since I'd seen *her* in some outlandish outfits.

Mom and Paige walked into the parlor. Paige's normally tan face looked sallow this morning, but her chest looked mighty impressive. Now that I knew Paige was pregnant, I could recognize the signs.

"Good morning," Mom said as she gave me a kiss on the cheek.

"How're you feeling, Paige?" I asked.

Paige smiled. "I've already thrown up twice, and I would kill for some caffeine. But I guess I'll make due with non-caffeinated hot tea."

I scrunched up my nose. "I'm sorry."

Paige sighed. "I know it will be worth it in the end, but right now I'm still trying to get used to peeing every ten minutes and looking over these top-heavy things." She gestured to her chest and I laughed.

Gary and Cybil Wainwright stepped into the parlor.

"Good morning," Gary Wainwright greeted. "I hope you slept well. As you can see, we've had a late arrival this morning. This is Wayne Skaggs, and he will be staying with us until tomorrow. Now let's make our way into the dining room where Bessie has prepared a lovely breakfast for us."

I looked around the room but didn't see Olivia Banner anywhere. Would she elect to stay in her room and not have breakfast this morning?

Wayne Skaggs stood up and walked over to where we were standing. I couldn't quite place it, but there was something about him that seemed familiar to me. I was sure I'd never met him, but something about the way he walked tugged on my memory.

Olivia Banner shuffled into the dining room just as breakfast was being served. She was unnaturally pale and her eyes were red rimmed. I smiled at her, but she didn't return the smile.

Once again we all sat in the same spots we had the previous night for dinner. Except for Wayne Skaggs…he now sat where Colonel Musgaard had sat. I had to wonder what happened to the slightly overweight older gentleman. Would we see him anymore during our stay?

Breakfast consisted of scrambled eggs, bacon, French toast with a homemade Bailey's whipped cream topping, and fresh berries. I'm not ashamed to say not only did I eat my serving of French toast, but I ate Paige's serving as well.

Once again Trent Starnes and Dayna Bowers helped with food service…and once again the tension between Trent and Dayna was palpable.

"Now don't forget," Gary Wainwright said once we had all been served and started eating, "Trent here will be out at the stables around ten if anyone wants to go horseback riding."

Tina tossed her hair as Trent leaned down to pour her more coffee. "I'd love for you to take me…for a ride."

Gag!

Trent was about as appealing as a month-old pork chop. Why in the world did the Wainwrights keep him on? Surely they could find someone else to take care of the horses.

"Stewie," Tina purred to her husband, "you don't mind if I let Trent take me for a ride, do you? You know how much I love horses."

Stewart Collins looked up absentmindedly from his phone. "What? Oh, right. Yes, have fun. I'm sure Trent can entertain you for the afternoon."

"I hope so," Tina whispered. I looked over at Olivia Banner. She was watching the exchange with disgust. Her white-knuckle grip on her fork left no doubt she'd love to stab Trent right through the heart.

Luckily Dayna was refilling a pitcher of orange juice in the kitchen and had missed the exchange. Something told me if she had heard it, Trent would be wearing the pitcher of orange juice.

"One last thing," Gary Wainwright said once we were finished with breakfast. "I expect the Sheriff to be here shortly to start taking statement from eyewitnesses for last night's murder of poor Colonel Musgaard."

Everyone started to slowly file out of the dining room. Paige wanted to rest up before we went horseback riding, so she and Mom went back up to their rooms. I noticed Aunt Shirley hadn't made a move to leave. Instead, she was staring intently at Wayne Skaggs.

"I must say," Aunt Shirley said, "it's quite remarkable."

Wayne Skaggs took a step backward. "What do you mean?"

Aunt Shirley chuckled. "You know what I mean." She looked around the room to make sure everyone else was gone. "The disguise. I wouldn't have recognized you if it hadn't been for the walk. The uneven gait must be natural."

Wayne Skaggs' mouth dropped open. "I've never had anyone, ever, put the two pieces together. How did you know?"

"Oh, you're good," Aunt Shirley said, "I'll give you that. But I used to be a private investigator. I notice all sorts of things."

I looked quizzically at Aunt Shirley. I had no idea what she was talking about, but it had Wayne Skaggs pretty shook up.

"Yeah, well, can you keep it our little secret?" Wayne asked. "It's part of the show."

"You bet." Aunt Shirley hooked her arms through mine. "Let's go see what books they have in the library before we go sign up for horseback riding."

We made our way to the other side of the house to the library. We'd just passed a partially closed door when I heard the Wainwrights talking. We must have stumbled upon their office. Out of habit, Aunt Shirley and I stopped to listen.

"Let's not worry about this right now, Cybil."

I heard sniffing and could tell Cybil Wainwright was crying. "You believe me, Gary, don't you? You know I'd never do that to you?"

Gary Wainwright sighed. "I do, Cybil. I don't know what's going on, but we will figure it out. Please don't cry anymore."

That seemed to cause Cybil Wainwright to cry even harder. I motioned with my head to keep walking. The library was one room down from Gary Wainwright's office.

"What do you suppose that was about?" I asked Aunt Shirley.

"I don't know. There seems to be a lot of sneaky stuff going on. And I don't think it has anything to do with the murder mystery. I think something big is going on."

"Speaking of the weekend murder mystery, what were you talking to Wayne Skaggs about?"

Aunt Shirley chuckled. "You didn't recognize him?"

I thought about that. "You know, something was familiar about him. I couldn't quite place it. I know I haven't met him before."

"If you put thirty more pounds on him, a receding hairline wig, and—"

"That was Colonel Musgaard!" I scrunched my forehead. "Wow, that was some change. He *is* good."

"Yes. I would have never recognized him if it wasn't for his walk. He has the same hitch in his left leg."

I nodded my head and smiled. "You really are good at this detective stuff, Aunt Shirley."

"You should have seen me back in my day. Now let's get some books and get out of here. I gotta go get my sexy on for the Sheriff!"

CHAPTER 6

I knocked on Mom and Paige's door and informed them I was going to go sign up for horseback riding. Aunt Shirley was still in the parlor flirting with Sheriff Simpson. He'd asked me a couple questions about what I witnessed and who I was with at the time the body was discovered. People had been acting so crazy this morning that I actually forgot we were in the middle of a pretend murder mystery.

The foyer was empty, so I peeked my head in the parlor to see if anyone was around. The parlor, like the foyer, was empty. For a place that was supposed to be putting on a pretend murder, people sure were missing in action a lot this morning.

I jogged out the front door and down the steps out to the barn. It was built to look like the house, complete with high pitched roofs with a cupola and weather vane. There were even shutters around the windows. Although, for me and my puny strength, the split sliding aisle doors were a bit awkward to open.

I rested—panting—against the door when Tina shot out from inside. She was adjusting her shirt as she walked past me. She giggled when she saw me and gave me a knowing wink.

I shoved past her without a word. While I didn't particularly like her husband, I especially didn't like the fact she would openly cheat on him with another guy. A guy that was supposed to be seeing another girl. This was turning out worse than those soap operas Aunt Shirley sometimes watched.

"Trent Starnes," I called out. "Are you in here?"

You pompous, arrogant jerk.

The first thing I noticed was the smell. Not gonna lie…it was a little overpowering. I may be from a small town, but I wasn't used to a horse barn smell. A combination of horse sweat, hay, poop, and leather. I made my way down the aisle of the barn. A horse peeked its head over the half stall he was in and neighed at me. I stopped and petted the horse's neck.

Trent popped his head out of the back office. "If it isn't the beautiful Ryli. What can I do for you this morning?" The leer on his face had my stomach rolling.

"I want to sign up four people for horseback riding. Can you handle that?"

"Sure. I can take the four of you on."

Gag. Where's a knife when I need it. I'd love to cut this jerk's tongue out.

Trent brought the rest of his body out the door and leaned suggestively against the frame. "How about you come back in about twenty minutes, okay? I have to get the horses around."

"Fine!" I snapped and stomped out of the stable. I really didn't want to spend the next hour and a half with this guy, but Aunt Shirley was looking forward to her birthday horseback ride.

I met Sheriff Simpson in the foyer. "Your aunt tells me it's her birthday today. Do you girls plan on doing something special?"

"In about twenty minutes, we're going for a nice horseback riding session and then maybe lunch in town. I honestly don't know when the next body is supposed to be found, so I guess we'll play it by ear."

Sheriff Simpson gave me a secretive smile. "I'd say you have time for a celebratory birthday lunch in town if you want." He gave me a conspiratorial wink. "I think I'm due to come back around four."

I laughed. "Good to know. Is Aunt Shirley upstairs?"

Sheriff Simpson nodded and shoved his cowboy hat back on his head. "Yes, Ma'am. Said she was going to go get gussied up for the horses."

"That sounds like Aunt Shirley. I guess I'll see you around four today," I said.

He tipped his hat to me and moseyed out the front door. I jogged up the stairs and roused Mom and Paige. I told them we'd meet them downstairs in the foyer in about fifteen minutes.

"Omigosh." I shut the bedroom door and looked at Aunt Shirley. "What is that?"

Aunt Shirley twirled. "You like? It's my riding outfit."

"Where—what—where…" I had no words.

She was standing in front of me in black leather skin-tight pants, a black leather button up vest with black lace sleeves, and black combat boots. She was also holding a riding crop whip. Only it wasn't a real riding crop whip…it was more of a prop…if you get my drift.

"I ran across this website called Leather Dreams and More or something like that. I don't quite remember. But it was on sale. So I had to have it!"

"When the outfit came to your house," I said, trying not to laugh, "was it wrapped in a brown bag with no markings on it?"

"How did you know?"

I suppressed a groan. Leave it to Aunt Shirley to stumble across a naughty website and not know.

"Well, I guess we better go on down to the stable." I couldn't wait to see Trent's reaction to this getup. Might put a damper on any other hanky-panky he had in mind…for the rest of the weekend!

I had to give Mom props. She only had a mild stroke when she took in Aunt Shirley's outfit. Paige, on the other hand, laughed until she nearly wet herself. I assured her I had the same reaction.

The four of us made our way out onto the back of the veranda and started down the stairs. I caught movement out of the corner of my eye and saw Dayna running around the back of the barn toward us. She was dressed in a black and red Lycra top and black Lycra shorts and running shoes. She looked out of breath as she hurried toward the front of the house. I raised my hand in greeting, but she didn't see me.

"I still can't believe you bought that crazy outfit," I said to Aunt Shirley as we walked into the barn. A huge anvil with tools scattered about took up a large chunk of room. Trent must have been checking the shoes on the horses. You'd think he'd put the tools back in their designated area. They had to be pretty expensive.

"Every celebration calls for a special outfit," Aunt Shirley bantered back.

"Mr. Starnes, are you here?" Mom called out.

A couple of the horses poked their noses out of the stalls as we strode down the aisle. I stopped to pet the one I had earlier. I had hoped Trent would have saddled her for me. I looked around the barn. There wasn't a single horse saddled and ready to ride.

"Mr. Starnes," Mom called again. "We're here for our riding session."

"Wait." Paige was bent over, her hands clasping her knees. "I'm not sure I can take the smell. Smells have really gotten to me lately."

"Honey, you don't have to go," Mom said gently. "I'll stay here with you. I remember being pregnant with Matt and every smell seemed to knock me over. I threw up every day for six months it seemed."

Paige lifted her head slightly. "I hope it's not like that for me."

"Yeah," I agreed, "don't do something that's gonna make you sick. Not worth it. I'm going to go see if Starnes is in his office."

I took off down the aisle and turned right at the end. I could see Starnes' office door was open. I looked down to make sure I wasn't stepping in anything unseemly when I noticed a body lying in the office doorway.

My startled scream was a natural reaction.

Trent Starnes was lying in a pool of blood with some sort of hammer next to his bludgeoned head.

"What in tarnation are you bellyaching about?" Aunt Shirley demanded as she strode toward me, her riding crop swinging back and forth as she walked. I tried to focus on that comical image so I wouldn't look at Trent Starnes's bloody body again.

"Hey," Aunt Shirley said when she got close enough to see Trent lying in the doorway. "I thought Sheriff Simpson said he wouldn't see me again until tonight." Aunt Shirley fluffed her hair in anticipation and then turned and hollered out to Mom and Paige.

"Come back here. We have another dead body. Only this one won't be hard to solve how he died. Got a…" Aunt Shirley trailed off and looked at Trent Starnes again. "Uh…he ain't pretend dead, is he?"

"No, he's not." I turned my head and sucked in two deep breaths. Mom and Paige were walking toward me. I held up my hands. "Don't come any closer. It's not a fake body. This one's real."

I heard Paige moan. "I need to go wait outside." She all but ran from the barn.

"How is it you are always stumbling over dead bodies?" Mom asked. "I just don't understand. Statistically speaking, it should be impossible."

I giggled. "I know, right. Garrett is gonna freak."

"Your momma is gonna freak." Mom said with a sigh. "I'll go find the Wainwrights."

"Hey, Nancy Drew," Aunt Shirley said, "go look through his office real quick before everyone arrives. See if you can find a clue."

I hesitated. I really didn't want to get involved. I just wanted to leave. I didn't want another chance at being held against my will, being drugged, being tormented. I just wanted to pack my bags and leave.

Aunt Shirley snapped her fingers. "I'm talking to you, girl. I'm about done searching his body."

I looked down at her rummaging through Trent's pockets. That got me moving. I carefully stepped over Trent's bloody body and into his office. It was a typical office as offices went. A mahogany desk with a standard office chair, a fairly new computer, and tons of bookshelves filled with books. I sat down in the chair and started opening drawers. I knew Mom would be back shortly, so I figured the desk was the best place to start.

I opened the two side drawers on my right. The top drawer held standard office supplies. Nothing helpful in there. I opened the bottom drawer and found files. I sifted through them but nothing caught my eye. They were standard invoices and receipts.

I looked up and was about to start looking through the bookshelves when a flash caught my eye. I squinted and looked at the bookshelf directly in front of me against the wall.

"Anything?" Aunt Shirley asked. She stood up and dusted off her black leather pants.

"Maybe. Come look at this." I walked to the bookshelf, peered down at the books, and located the flash that caught my eye. Sandwiched between two large books was a slim camcorder. The largest thing on it was the camera eye. It was the same color as the two books it was sandwiched between, so no one would notice unless they knew what to look for.

I pulled it out and held it in my hand. It weighed about the same as my cell phone. I flipped open the lid and pushed the stop button.

"It's one of those pocket camcorders," Aunt Shirley said. "We definitely need to see what's on that tape."

"It's back here." Mom's voice reverberated in the quiet barn.

I started to put the camcorder back where I found it when Aunt Shirley grabbed my arm. "Keep it."

"No!" In a panic I shoved the camcorder at Aunt Shirley. "You keep it!"

"You're sure he's dead?" Gary Wainwright asked. Their voices sounded close.

"I got nowhere to store it," Aunt Shirley insisted, shoving the camcorder back at me. "These leather pants are really tight!"

My heart was practically leaping out of my chest. They were four steps from the door and Aunt Shirley and I were still playing hot potato with the camcorder.

"Put it down your shirt," I hissed. "You've had a flask down there before. This is even smaller."

"True." Aunt Shirley quickly unbuttoned the top two buttons on the leather vest, dropped the camcorder in her bra, then hastily buttoned the vest back up.

"No!" Gary Wainwright gasped. "It *is* Trent!"

Aunt Shirley and I turned to the doorway as Gary Wainwright knelt down by the body. He reached out to pick up the hammer.

"Don't touch that!" Aunt Shirley cried. "There could be fingerprints on it."

"Oh, right." Gary stood up looking dazed. "I can't believe this. I guess I better call Sheriff Simpson."

"No offense," I said. "But I think we need a real Sheriff, not one of your actors."

Gary Wainwright frowned and then gave me a weak smile. "Actually, Sheriff Simpson *is* a real Sheriff. He's usually slow most days. It's not like these parts see a lot of criminal activity out here. He drops in when he knows we need him during our murder mystery weekends."

Gary called Sheriff Simpson to tell him what had happened, and then suggested Mom, Aunt Shirley, and I go back inside the house to wait. He'd stay with the body to make sure nothing happened to it. Without accusing him of tampering—which we'd just done—there was nothing we could do but go back to the house and wait.

I carefully stepped over the body again and looked to my left. I hadn't noticed the door there before. "Where does that door lead?"

Gary Wainwright looked where I pointed. "That's just a back door to the barn. More of an emergency door. No one really uses it."

We carefully made our way out of the barn and I blinked my eyes a few times to get used to the glare of the sun.

"I want to look at something real quick," I said.

Mom groaned. "What?"

"Just follow me," I said.

I led them around the back of the barn. It was the beginning of the walking trail the brochure had mentioned…five acres of woods and trails to explore. It was also where the back door of the barn opened up. My stomach sank. "Do you guys remember when we were going out to the barn and we saw Dayna? She came from this back area. I guess she could have been walking the trails in the woods, but…"

"But she could also have been coming back from beating Trent Starnes over the head," Aunt Shirley finished.

"Now wait just a second," Mom interjected. "That's a pretty big leap."

"But look how upset she's been over his behavior," I said. "Plus she was wearing black so there's no way to tell right now if there was blood on the clothes. And I'm not saying she did it—"

"Good," Mom said firmly.

"But she very well could be our number one suspect," Aunt Shirley said.

"Leave it alone," Mom warned. "Let the police handle this."

"Sure thing, Janine." Aunt Shirley looked at me and winked.

CHAPTER 7

Just like last night, Sheriff Simpson arrived within a few minutes of the nine-one-one call. He immediately ushered us all into the parlor while the emergency crew took care of Trent Starnes's body in the barn.

"Don't forget to watch reactions," Aunt Shirley whispered to me as she crossed in front of me to stand on the opposite side of the room.

Dayna Bowers sat on the couch in between her aunt and uncle. "I just can't believe this," Dayna sniffed as she wiped a tear from her cheek.

Sheriff Simpson held up his hand. "Folks, I want each of you to take a seat, please."

The cook, Bessie Terrance, strode angrily into the parlor. "What's this about? I'm in the middle of preparing lunch. If I don't get back to the kitchen it will burn."

Tina Collins sat on the fireplace hearth chewing on her fingernail and shooting daggers at her husband. Stewart Collins was on the phone yelling and telling the other person he wouldn't be able to make his meeting because some imbecile went and got himself murdered and now no one could leave.

You're all heart, Stewart.

"Sir," Sheriff Simpson hollered at Stewart, "I'm not telling you again to get off the phone. Next time I do, I'm confiscating the phone."

Stewart promptly hung up and scowled down at his wife. He elected to stand while she sat chewing her nails.

Wayne Skaggs was sitting in the overstuffed chair next to the fireplace. Every so often he'd run his hands through his hair and mutter to himself.

"I don't suppose we have any champagne?" Olivia Banner asked as she made her way to the bar cart located by the wall where Aunt Shirley was standing. When no one answered, she picked up a glass tumbler and poured some whiskey into it. She took a long swallow and smiled at me.

"Like I've already said, I have my deputies on this urgent matter," Sheriff Simpson said, "but until we get a chance to talk to all parties, I'm going to ask that you not leave the premises unless I give you permission."

Stewart Collins started cursing at his wife. "You better hope this gets resolved by tomorrow, because I'm not calling in Monday to work over a stupid murder we know nothing about." He strode angrily for the door. "I'll be in my room working if anyone wishes to find me."

I glanced over at the Wainwrights. Even though Cybil was comforting Dayna, I could tell she was only half into it. Interestingly, both Cybil and Gary didn't look upset by the murder, they looked worried.

Are they worried because they're afraid of losing customers? Or could it have something to do with what Gary and Cybil were whispering about in Gary's office this morning?

"I'll leave you all to either retire to your rooms or move about freely in the house," Sheriff Simpson said. "Again, please do not leave the confines of the house. Aunt Shirley and Ryli, may I speak to you in the library, please?"

I figured it made sense he'd want to talk with us first, since we did discover the body. We followed him out of the parlor, through the foyer, and down the corridor into the library. I sat down in one of the chairs.

"I'll keep this brief," Sheriff Simpson said. "I know you both have experience working crime scenes."

We do?

"What I'm about to ask you to do is not unheard of. I'd appreciate it if you could infiltrate the troops and maybe try to pick up on some information I might not be privy to. They'll probably open up to you two more than they will me." Sheriff Simpson took off his cowboy hat and ran his hand over his head. "I don't want you looking for clues, or taking it upon yourself to solve this case, mind you…but just talk to the others, see what they have to say."

Aunt Shirley's face lit up. "You bet we will. Ryli and I are pretty good at solving murders. What's this make now, Ryli? Three or four?"

I closed my eyes and shook my head. I wanted no part of this, but I knew it wouldn't matter. "I don't know, Aunt Shirley. I've lost count."

Aunt Shirley patted Sheriff Simpson's arm. "Well, never you mind, Sheriff. Ryli and I are on this for you."

Sheriff Simson furrowed his brow. "Well, now, like I said, I don't want you doing any actual investigating, just talking."

"Of course," Aunt Shirley said reassuringly. "We won't try and solve the case. We'll just talk with the others."

I knew there wasn't a bit of truth in what she'd just said.

Sheriff Simpson shoved his hat back on his head then tipped his hat to us. "Thank you, ladies. Now, tell me about the body you found."

****

After we spoke to Sheriff Simpson, he left us alone in the library so he could go question the others. I picked up a pen and paper and started making a suspect list and motives. I'd just started the list when Aunt Shirley and I heard excited voices coming from next door.

"That's the private office," I said.

"Let's go see what's going on."

I sighed and picked up the pen and paper I'd snagged from one of the library end tables. I could already tell it was going to be a long day.

We stood in the hallway and put our ear against the door, hoping to hear something.

I could only make out Gary Wainwright's every second or third word. "Burn…pictures…ever know."

"I say we go in." Aunt Shirley knocked on the door and then turned the knob before they even told us to come in.

"We heard some of what you just said," Aunt Shirley declared. "And I think we need to talk."

Gary Wainwright was standing resolute behind his desk. A handful of pictures were scattered in front of him. He frowned at Aunt Shirley. "This is a private matter between me and my wife. I'm afraid I need to ask you to leave."

Cybil was sitting in a chair in front of the desk, wiping her eyes with a tissue. "Let them come in, Gary. We have nowhere else to turn. We can't keep hiding."

"We heard mention of pictures," Aunt Shirley said from the doorway. "What pictures?"

Gary Wainwright handed me the photos on his desk. I flipped through them, but it didn't take me long to see they were pretty scandalous. The man's back was to me, but I could make out the side of his face. There was no denying it was Trent Starnes. The woman's face and body, even though facing the camera, was hard to make out. The only thing I could see for sure was the flowered dress and brown, wavy hair.

"Is this you?" I gently asked Cybil Wainwright.

Cybil started crying again. "I swear to you, it's not. I don't know how this has happened. I mean, it's my dress, but that's not me. I wasn't sleeping with Trent Starnes."

A gasp sounded behind Aunt Shirley. "You were sleeping with Trent?" Dayna cried. "How could you?"

Aunt Shirley reached out and grabbed Dayna, hauling her inside the room. "Oops. Sorry about that. I should have made sure the door was closed."

"I can't believe this!" Dayna cried. "It's bad enough I had to watch Trent hook up with every woman that came here, but my own *aunt*! You should be—"

"That's enough!" Gary Wainwright ordered. "Dayna, I believe Cybil when she says she was not sleeping with Trent."

"May I see the pictures?" Aunt Shirley said.

Gary handed the photos to Aunt Shirley. She flipped through them without saying a word. "When did they arrive?"

"Yesterday," Cybil whispered. "They came in the mail. Only with everyone arriving and such, I forgot to remind Gary to check his mail. It wasn't until this morning that we saw them."

I thought back to when I first overheard them talking about the pictures. It had been this morning after breakfast and before I went out to talk with Trent about the horseback riding. I remember thinking that the house was eerily quiet and no one was around.

"No!" Dayna's hands flew up to her mouth as she stared at the pictures. "Where did you get these pictures?"

"These are the pictures that were addressed to me," Gary Wainwright said. "I'm assuming Trent sent them."

"Why do you assume Trent sent them?" I asked.

"Well, who else would send me pictures of Trent and Cybil…doing this?"

"That's not Aunt Cybil," Dayna whispered. "That's me!"

We all turned and stared at the girl. She carried the pictures with her and sat down in the chair opposite her aunt. "I remember this day. I had just finished my morning chores and was going to retire to my room until the lunch hour rush. I opened my bedroom door and there was a note slipped under the door from Trent. It said to change into a pretty dress with flowers on it and he'd take me on a walk before lunch. I remember he specifically asked me to change into a pretty dress with flowers like the one my aunt had, only he knew I didn't have a dress like that. So I sneaked into Aunt Cybil's room and borrowed the dress." The young girl turned to her aunt. "I'm so sorry I thought it was you." She put her hands over her face and started to cry. "I'm so ashamed and embarrassed."

Cybil Wainwright got up from her chair and enveloped the sobbing girl in her arms. "Oh, honey. I'm the one that's sorry. I'm sorry that rotten man ever got anywhere near you. I'm so sorry he obviously used you."

"There was a letter that came with the photos." Gary reached under his desk and pulled out a middle drawer. He rummaged around in the back before pulling it out. "I didn't want anyone to find it."

He handed the note to Aunt Shirley. She read it aloud. "Just a little hint of what your wife does when you aren't around. Put five thousand dollars cash in the enclosed envelope and put it in the mail. I want the money by next week."

"Why just five thousand dollars?" I asked Aunt Shirley. "If he was blackmailing them, why not ask for more?"

"I'd say because he was demanding payment immediately," Aunt Shirley said. "He couldn't ask for too much because then it would take a while to get. Something tells me the Wainwrights aren't the only ones he was blackmailing."

I sighed and did my best to soften the blow. "Dayna, I'm sorry to ask you this, but I saw you running from the back of the barn area this morning. It was right around the time we discovered the body. What were you doing back there?"

Cybil Wainwright gasped and Dayna scowled at me. "I wasn't in the barn. I was out for my morning walk. There's a trail back behind the barn I like to walk. I do it most mornings. You can ask anyone!"

Cybil Wainwright stroked her niece's hair. "Shhh, baby. No one thinks you killed Trent."

Hmmm...I wouldn't go that far.

"And just because all bases will need to be covered," Aunt Shirley said. "What about you two? I mean, you discover this note, and yet a lot of time passed. Why didn't you confront Trent? Because if I got pictures like this in the mail, I'd be seeking some vengeance immediately."

Cybil and Gary looked at each other before Gary spoke. "I'll admit my first reaction was to go throttle the boy. But then we started to panic. Cybil and I agreed we'd give him the money and then fire him. We were in this room the whole time this morning trying to figure out a way to come up with the cash quickly."

"Can I see the envelope you were supposed to send the money in?" Aunt Shirley asked.

"Sure." Gary rummaged around on his desk for a few seconds and then pulled out a large manila envelope. "Here it is."

"The name is John Smith, but it's a P.O. Box," Aunt Shirley said. "This pretty much solidifies it for me that you guys weren't the only ones he's been blackmailing. He sends evidence out to a few women and their husbands and then demands small payments to a P.O. Box." Aunt Shirley looked at the address closer. "Where is this town, Millsap? Is it around here?"

Cybil nodded. "Yes, it's about thirty minutes from here."

I suddenly remembered the camera in Aunt Shirley's bra! Things had been so crazy that we hadn't had time to look at it, much less turn it over to Sheriff Simpson. We really needed to get to our rooms and watch it. If luck was on our side, the killer would be on the tape.

CHAPTER 8

"So what did Sheriff Simpson say to you two?" Paige asked as Aunt Shirley and I walked into their bedroom a few minutes later.

Mom was sitting on the bed refolding clothes. A sure sign she was upset. "He didn't ask for your help, did he?"

"He sure did!" Aunt Shirley exclaimed. "Said he heard about how we're always solving murders. I told him not to worry, we were on it."

I suppressed a smile when Mom closed her eyes and shook her head. "Don't worry, Mom. He only asked us to talk with the people here. He warned us we were not to do any actual investigating, just talking. And, really, how much trouble can we get into? You'll be here to make sure we don't do anything foolish."

Mom scoffed. "I was with you at Paige's bachelorette party. And we all remember how that turned out, right?"

I scooted the folded clothes over so I wouldn't sit on them. "I promise we won't do anything too crazy, okay? I know how much you worry."

"And I'll be watching over the girl," Aunt Shirley added. No surprise Mom let out a huge groan.

Paige giggled then winked at me. "Not exactly the shining endorsement your mom was hoping for."

"We're gonna go to our room," I said. "Since it looks like Aunt Shirley's birthday lunch is out, how about we meet down in the parlor for lunch." I checked the clock on my cell phone. "Say in twenty minutes?"

"Sure," Mom agreed.

Aunt Shirley and I retreated to our room. I was anxious to view the camcorder, and with only twenty minutes until lunch, I knew we had to be fast.

"Let's see it," I said as I stuck my hand out to Aunt Shirley.

"Hold on." I watched in fascinating disgust as Aunt Shirley reached down and dug around in her bra. "Eureka!"

I suppressed a gag as she handed the hot, sweaty box to me. We sat down on the bed next to each other, neither one of us saying a word as I flipped open the top and started rewinding the digital recorder. When it stopped I pushed play. We both leaned forward.

Then immediately leaned back in disgust.

"Ugh! I was *not* prepared for that!" I cried.

Aunt Shirley shook her head in wonder. "I haven't seen anything like that in…well, in many, many years."

"Stop!" I begged. "I can't take any more."

The image on the screen was of Tina Collins and Trent Starnes, and what they were doing was straight up illegal I was sure. I rubbed my palms over my eyes, hoping to erase the image that seemed to be burned into my brain.

"Guess she was right," Aunt Shirley snickered. "She went out there to get her ride on and she—"

"Enough!" I slapped Aunt Shirley playfully on the arm. "I feel like I should be gouging out my eyeballs."

66

"Let's see what else is on there. Fast forward it a little bit."

I did as Aunt Shirley requested, and we both got the giggles when the images on the screen started doing the nasty at warp speed.

When the images on the screen became G-rated again, I slowed the camera down. Tina was leaving the office and Trent was walking toward the camera. He cursed and moved back away from the camera and called out.

"That's my voice!" I said as I paused the video. "I met Tina coming out of the barn and she was adjusting her clothes. Then I went in and called out to Trent. He said to give him twenty minutes and he'd have the horses ready."

I pushed play again. Trent walked back into the office and went to sit at his desk. Obviously he'd forgotten about turning off the camera when I startled him. I heard a noise off camera and saw Trent's head jerk up. He looked over at the door and scowled. Unfortunately, the camera only gave a visual of his desk so we couldn't see who it was.

"What do you want?" Trent said as he got up and went toward the door. "I told you—"

Aunt Shirley and I jumped at the sound of Trent's head taking the blow. My hands started to shake. We couldn't see anything, but we could hear Trent crying out in pain. Then silence.

Aunt Shirley and I sat there on the bed breathing hard. I fast forwarded the tape a few more minutes and then let it play. A couple seconds later I heard my voice again.

"This must be when the four of us came back into the barn and discovered the body," I said. We listened to the rest of the story unfold…Aunt Shirley telling me to go inside the office and look for clues. I saw me sit down at Trent's desk and open drawers. Then my face up close and personal as I picked the camera up off the shelf and turned it off.

I blew out a breath. "That's it. Nothing really there except some nasty stuff no one should ever have to see, and then the murder. We don't hear or see anything that helps us."

Aunt Shirley chewed on her bottom lip. "We really don't. I guess the next time we see Sheriff Simpson, we'll give this to him. We'll tell him we forgot to give it to him in the excitement if he asks."

I looked at my cell phone. "We better head on down for lunch."

"I need to change out of this outfit. It's not really all that comfortable." Aunt Shirley grabbed a pair of polyester pants and a floral button-up blouse out of the dresser. "Oh, and don't think I haven't noticed that you haven't texted your boyfriend and told him about what's happened."

I groaned. "Don't remind me. I'm kinda hoping we have some good solid leads when I call him tonight. This way he doesn't give me too much grief."

Aunt Shirley hooted on her way to the bathroom to change. "Good luck with that!"

***

Lunch was a light affair of fruit salad, grilled cheese sandwiches, cranberry muffins, and sweet tea. Everyone was in attendance but Tina and Stewart Collins. I had to wonder if Stewart didn't suspect something. I was going to make it my mission to find Tina and talk with her. Especially since I've seen more of that woman up front and personal than I have of Paige. And Paige has been my best friend for almost thirty years!

"I think I'm going to go to the library and see what I can find," Mom said after lunch. "Maybe read and take a nap."

"That sounds great," Paige said. "Can I come, too?"

"You bet." Mom pushed her chair back to leave when Wayne put his hand on her arm.

"I'd love to talk books if you have a little time," he said. "Not only am I an avid reader, but I'm currently writing a novel."

I could tell Mom wasn't keen on the idea, but she must have realized Wayne was only being friendly and probably bored out of his mind, because she agreed.

The three of them left to go to the library. Gary and Cybil Wainwright excused themselves for the office to take care of paperwork, and Dayna followed closely behind. The poor girl still looked like death warmed over.

"Well," Olivia said, "I'm in the mood to party. Do you want to join me in the parlor for a little whiskey and gossip?"

Gossip, yes…whiskey, no.

"I think that would be nice," Aunt Shirley said.

Of course you do!

Aunt Shirley and I followed Olivia into the parlor and waited patiently as she poured each of us a glass of whiskey and went to sit down.

"I can't help but notice that you've been in a pretty chipper mood since they discovered Trent's body," Aunt Shirley said before taking a sip of her drink.

Olivia laughed humorlessly. "You bet I am. This couldn't have happened to a better person." She knocked back a little of her drink. "I know how that sounds, but I just don't care. I've thought about killing that SOB for months. I just didn't think I'd have the good fortune to actually see it happen."

Aunt Shirley didn't say anything, but I could tell she was taking in everything Olivia said. "Do you think you and your husband will be able to get back together now?"

Olivia's mouth dropped open. "How did you know we weren't together anymore?" Her eyes filled with tears but she blinked them back. "I only told the Wainwrights he was working and I wanted to get away."

Aunt Shirley clucked her tongue. "You've been miserable. Your eyes have been swollen like you've been crying for days. And my niece here saw you and Trent arguing early this morning and you slapped him."

Olivia paled and lifted a shaking hand to take another drink. Unfortunately there wasn't a whole lot left in her glass. She got up and poured herself another.

"I'm all for drowning sorrows, dear." Aunt Shirley said. "But you're gonna want to keep a level head about you until this murder is solved."

Olivia sat down again on the couch and this time took a little sip of her whiskey. "It's true. I did confront Trent this morning, and I did slap him."

"Was he blackmailing you?" I asked. I knew Cybil couldn't be his first time.

Olivia barked out a laugh. "Yes!" She leaned over and grabbed a wad of tissue out of the box. "About three months ago I came here to Mystery Farms with my husband. We were already having some problems in the marriage, and so when Trent came on to me, I went for it." She paused and wiped her nose. "I thought it would be a one-time thing and my husband, Brian, would never know. Then about two months ago, I got an envelope in the mail. There were pictures of me and Trent in some very compromising positions."

I knew those positions all too well. I had unfortunately witnessed them between Tina and Trent just an hour or two ago.

"So, I did what Trent requested and I sent him a thousand dollars in the envelope. I thought that would be the end of it."

"But it wasn't?" Aunt Shirley prompted.

Olivia sighed. "No. I received another envelope demanding more money a couple weeks later. It was never for huge amounts, but enough that it was beginning to break me. But I was willing to do it to keep him quiet. Until…"

"Until he sent pictures to your husband?" Aunt Shirley guessed.

Olivia said nothing, just nodded her head. "Brian was so angry. He wanted to know who it was. I guess he didn't recognize or remember Trent. I was afraid if Brian found out who it was, he would kill him!"

You don't say?

"So I told Brian I would take care of it. Brian said I had one week to settle it or he'd leave me forever." Olivia hiccupped. "I know sleeping with Trent was wrong, and I'm really sorry. I don't want to lose my husband. I came here to put a stop to the blackmail."

"How exactly were you going to do that?" I asked.

Olivia shrugged. "I thought if I confronted him and told him that my husband and I would sue him for harassment, he might back off."

"Do you still have the latest blackmail request and envelope?" Aunt Shirley asked. "I'd like to look at it if you do."

Olivia nodded. "Yes. It's in my room. Do you want me to slip it under your door when I find it?"

"That would be great," I said.

"Have you spoken to your husband about what has happened here?" Aunt Shirley asked. "About Trent being murdered?"

Olivia bit her lip. "That's the thing. I've been trying to call him since Trent's body was discovered, but he's not answering his phone. I can't seem to reach him."

My eyes felt like they were gonna pop out of my head. "When's the last time you spoke to your husband?"

Olivia dug out her phone. "Yesterday after I got here and right before dinner. We had a terrible fight. I found out he's at my mom's house."

"Does your mom know what's happened?" Aunt Shirley asked.

"Yes. And I made her promise not to tell Brian where I was. But he can be very persuasive and charming when he needs to be." Olivia gave a hallow laugh. "I wouldn't be surprised if he knows by now where I'm staying. I just wanted to confront Trent, make him stop, and get out of here before Brian figured things out. Jealous husbands are never a good thing."

"Ain't that the truth," Aunt Shirley said.

I barely suppressed a laugh.

"Speaking of jealous husbands," Olivia said. "You might want to check out Stewart Collins. I wouldn't be surprised if he actually knew what was going on between Trent and his wife. This whole I-hate-the-world-leave-me-alone-I-work-for-a-living thing could be a disguise."

Aunt Shirley smiled. "I've had the same thought, my dear. Jealous husbands will do all sorts of crazy things."

"And that's why you confronted Trent this morning by the barn?" I asked.

Olivia nodded. "Yes. Only…it was really weird. When I confronted him about the pictures and the money, he acted like he had no idea what I was talking about!"

CHAPTER 9

Aunt Shirley and I left Olivia to drown her sorrows and headed for the kitchen to talk with Bessie Terrance. Aunt Shirley and I ran into Mom and Paige coming out of the library.

"Enjoy your time with Wayne?" I teased.

Mom grimaced. "He's a nice enough guy, but I can't take being in his presence for long. He loves to hear the sound of his own voice."

Paige giggled. "We did learn a lot about him."

We parted ways and went to go find Bessie. We found her sitting at a tiny table in the middle of the kitchen writing down a list of supplies she was in need of. "Something I can get for you ladies?"

"Actually," Aunt Shirley said, "we were hoping to talk with you about Trent Starnes."

Bessie stopped writing and turned to us, a scowl on her face. "Look, I'll tell you the same thing I told the Sheriff. I don't know anything. The boy was a horn dog. Went sniffing around every woman that came here. Broke poor Miss Dayna's heart. But I don't know who would want to go and kill him."

"Where were you this morning around the time the body was discovered?" Aunt Shirley asked.

Bessie blew her red, frizzy hair out of her eyes. "Why? I already answered Sheriff Simpson's questions. Don't see why I need to answer you."

I put my hand on Bessie's arm. "Maybe you saw something important but you don't know it's important. If you tell us where you were, we can mark it on our timeline."

"Fine. I was busy cleaning the kitchen. That means I was in the kitchen and sometimes I was upstairs in the west wing in the laundry room putting the dirty linens from breakfast in the wash."

Aunt Shirley frowned. "That seems like a terrible place to put a laundry room. You have to haul all that laundry out through the dining room, foyer, up the stairs and to the west wing?"

Bessie laughed. "Heavens no. I'm too old to do all that." She turned and pointed to a skinny door by the refrigerator. "See that door? Behind it is what used to be called a servant's staircase. Basically it's a back entrance that dumps out into the west wing."

Aunt Shirley brightened. "I remember Dayna telling us that all guests stay on the east wing when we first got here. So, who stays on the west wing?"

"The staff. Trent, Wayne Skaggs, and me. There are two bedrooms located downstairs away from the main part of the house, and that's where Mr. and Mrs. Wainwright and Miss Dayna sleep."

"Did you see anyone upstairs in the west wing when you went up there this morning?"

"The only person up there would be Wayne. And I didn't see him, but I did hear him."

I frowned. "Hear him? What do you mean?"

Bessie rolled her eyes. "That man is always writing on a novel when he's not doing his acting bit here. He thinks he's the next Hemingway."

"What exactly *does* Wayne do here?" Aunt Shirley asked.

"He plays two different characters in the play on the weekends, and during the week he helps out with lawn care and other maintenance. Same as Trent when Trent wasn't taking care of the horses."

"And how exactly did you hear him?" I asked.

"That man refuses to get into the modern age. He still insists on plunking away on some antique typewriter. You know, the kind that makes loud sounds and dings. Blasted thing keeps me up some nights. I've had to learn to sleep with earbuds in my ears!"

Aunt Shirley looked toward the narrow door. "Could we go up and see Trent's room?"

Bessie shrugged. "I don't have a key, but I know Mr. Wainwright does."

"Thanks," Aunt Shirley said. "We'll go find Mr. Wainwright and see if we can't get into his room. You've been a big help, Bessie."

We left Bessie and went in search of the Wainwrights. Aunt Shirley's cell phone vibrated. She pulled it out and looked at it.

"It's from Sheriff Simpson. He said there's been a terrible accident on Hwy 19 and he won't be able to get back to Mystery Farms until later this evening. He wants to know if we have anything new to report."

Aunt Shirley hunched over her phone and started clicking away like a mad woman.

There was no one behind the front desk when we walked into the foyer, or anywhere else in the vicinity for that matter.

"I wonder where Mr. Wainwright is?" I asked.

"Who knows," Aunt Shirley said without looking up from the phone. "Get back there and grab a key from the box on the wall. If we're lucky the rooms are labeled."

"Why do I have to be the one to steal the key? Why don't you do it?"

Aunt Shirley looked up from her phone and huffed. "Because I need to be quick on my feet if we get caught. I'm good at getting us out of jams."

She had me there.

"Fine," I sighed. I slowly made my way around the counter. I took a quick look over my shoulder, saw the coast was clear, then quietly opened the wooden box on the wall that contained the keys to all the rooms.

Luck was with me. I spotted a row that had the employees' names on them with a key on the hook. I reached for Trent's key when I heard Aunt Shirley let out a squeak. "Get down! Hide! It's Wainwright."

I heard the front door open and quickly shut the door to the wooden box then dropped down to my hands and knees. I scrambled across the floor and pressed up against the counter as much as I could. I turned my head to the right and spotted the antacids Dayna had given me recently, along with a First-Aid kit. I willed my heart to stop pounding as I tried to control my breathing.

"Aunt Shirley," Mr. Wainwright said. "Is there something I can help you with?"

Aunt Shirley started to moan. "My heart! I think I'm having a heart attack!"

"Oh, no! Let me grab the phone behind the counter. I'll call nine-one-one for you!"

"No!" Aunt Shirley screamed. "I mean, I think if I rest in the parlor a moment I'll be okay."

"I don't think resting is going to stop a heart attack," Mr. Wainwright replied.

"Maybe it's not a heart attack," Aunt Shirley said quickly. "I bet it's gas. I've been awful gassy lately."

Mr. Wainwright coughed. "Oh. Well, in that case, maybe lying down for a minute in the parlor will do the trick."

"Will you help me to the parlor? I fear I may not make it there on my own."

"Of course," Mr. Wainwright said.

A few seconds later their voices tapered off and it was silent once again. I popped up quickly from behind the counter and made a dash for the wooden box. My hands were shaking as I yanked the box open, grabbed Trent's keys off the hook, and slammed the box shut.

I stuff the key in my pocket and took off for the parlor to relieve Aunt Shirley.

"Are you sure you're feeling better already?" Mr. Wainwright said as I entered the parlor. He was waving his hand under his nose.

"Yep. I think it was the way I sat down on the couch. Just enough pressure on my tummy and out that toot came. See, no heart attack, just gas."

"Yes, well. I guess that's good." Mr. Wainwright slowly backed up from Aunt Shirley. "If that's all you need, I better go see to a few things. I'm glad you're feeling better." He turned on his heels, mumbled hello to me, and fled from the room.

"You're a nasty woman," I grinned.

Aunt Shirley shrugged. "Farting on demand comes in handy sometimes."

"I got the key," I said. "Let's go by our room real quick and see if Olivia gave us the blackmail letter, and then we'll sneak over to Trent's room."

"Sounds good."

We walked up the stairs and Aunt Shirley received a text on her phone. She read it, giggled, and sent a reply. Seeing as how she had a slight flush to her, I figured she was bordering on sending indecent texts to the unsuspecting Sheriff Simpson. I didn't say a word, just guided her up the stairs and to our room.

I unlocked the door and bent down to retrieve a note. It was the letter and envelope Olivia said she'd slide under the door.

"Let's see the paper." Aunt Shirley put her hand out and I placed the letter and envelope in her hand. It was high-end stationery. Not exactly expensive, but not cheap, thin stuff either. "Notice anything about the paper?"

I nodded. "It's the same paper that was sent to both Olivia *and* the Wainwrights."

Aunt Shirley smiled. "Remember where we saw this paper?"

I frowned. "No. Have we seen this before?"

"Just today, in fact."

I thought back to everything we'd seen. I remembered! "Yes. Bessie was writing her grocery list on paper like this!"

Aunt Shirley chuckled. "She was indeed. Looking more and more like Sheriff Simpson is gonna need his handcuffs…and not just for me!"

I slapped my hands over my ears. "Geez! Must you, Aunt Shirley? I…can't…even!"

Aunt Shirley slapped me on my shoulder and I pitched forward. I really needed to start working out. When a septuagenarian can almost bring you to your knees with a slap, you know you're in trouble.

***

"Hurry," I hissed and looked quickly down both sides of the hallway in the west wing. "I don't want to get caught."

Aunt Shirley stuck Trent's key in the lock and pushed open his door.

"We're in," Aunt Shirley whispered. "Let's go."

We slipped into the room and quietly closed the door. The room was pretty much laid out like ours, only a tiny bit smaller. There was a queen-sized bed, a dresser, a small dressing area, and bathroom. A pint-sized secretary was pushed up against the wall.

"You rummage through his drawers," Aunt Shirley snickered at her crude joke, "and I'll check the secretary."

I pulled open the top drawer to the dresser and dug through Trent's underwear and socks. Not exactly the most glamorous job I've ever had—but not exactly the worst job, either. When I didn't find anything, I shut the drawer and opened the next one. I continued until I'd gone through everything.

"I didn't find anything relevant," I said.

Aunt Shirley looked up from the secretary. "I did." She waved the same stationery used to write the blackmail letters in the air.

I sighed dejectedly. "Yes. But we figured Trent was the one writing the letters and asking for money, why else would he have been killed?"

Aunt Shirley pursed her lips. "I've been thinking about that. I think it could have gone one of two ways. Either Trent sent everyone blackmail letters and someone here finally killed him…or someone is going to great lengths to frame Trent." Aunt Shirley shook her head. "No. Now that I've said it aloud it sounds too far-fetched. I still think someone here killed Trent because he blackmailed the wrong person."

"But you heard Olivia say when she confronted Trent he acted like he didn't know anything about the blackmail. So maybe it's not too far-fetched after all."

Aunt Shirley grunted. "You'd really have to hate someone to set them up for something like this. Maybe we need to take another look at Trent's past."

I opened Trent's door and ran straight into Wayne Skaggs. "Hey there, pretty lady. What're you doing in Trent's room?"

I tried not to grimace too much at the smarmy compliment.

"The Sheriff asked us to get something out of Trent's room," I lied.

"That's right. I heard you two were some sort of super sleuths or something like that."

I laughed but Aunt Shirley answered. "You bet we are. And while we're here, we have some questions for you." She paused dramatically. "Unless there's a reason you don't want to answer some questions?"

Wayne smiled and spread his arms wide. "I'm an open book. Ask me anything."

Aunt Shirley folded her arms across her sagging chest and gave Wayne the stink eye. "Okay. How long had you known Trent?"

Wayne looked up toward the ceiling then shrugged. "I don't know. I guess about a year now. I was hired a year and a half ago as an actor and attendant, if you will. The Wainwrights have only been doing the murder mystery theater that long. Then about a year ago Trent showed up. Gary had put out an ad looking for a horse trainer and caretaker."

"Do you know where Trent came from?" I asked.

Wayne pursed his lips in thought. "Well, I think I remember him saying something about Wyoming. Like maybe he worked on a horse ranch in Wyoming. I bet Mr. Wainwright could help you out more."

"Did you like Trent?" Aunt Shirley asked. "As a person, did you like him?"

"He was a likeable enough guy. He was charismatic, had a way with the ladies, but…"

"But what?" I asked.

"Well, let's just say I didn't always agree with his treatment of women. And then when he started seeing Miss Dayna, I knew that wasn't going to end well."

"I wonder why Gary and Cybil let that relationship happen?" I asked.

Wayne shrugged. "Well, I don't think at first they knew. I think the youngins kept it quiet for a while. Then by the time it came to light, I guess the Wainwrights figured it would be okay."

"Thanks for the information," Aunt Shirley said. "Guess we will see you for dinner."

Wayne's eyes lit up. "I had a great talk with your mom today. I'm thinking of asking her to take a stroll with me after dinner tonight."

Oh, boy. I'm not touching that with a ten-foot pole.

CHAPTER 10

"Let's make one more stop before we get ready for dinner tonight," Aunt Shirley said as we headed toward our room.

"To talk to Stewart?" I guessed.

Aunt Shirley grinned. "You got it. See if his blustering is just a ruse."

The door to the Hercule Poirot room was not fully shut as we passed by, and we heard voices inside. I recognized Olivia's voice, but the other voice belonged to a man.

"You're sure you knew nothing about this?" Olivia asked.

"I swear, no!" the man said. "Once your mom finally told me where you were, I hopped in the car and drove the three hours here. I turned off my phone just in case you tried to call because I wanted to surprise you. I love you, Olivia. I came here to save our marriage. And I came here to confront that piece of —"

"Shhh," Olivia said. "It doesn't matter anymore because he's dead."

No one said anything for a few seconds.

"Olivia's husband Brian?" I whispered to Aunt Shirley.

"I assume so," she whispered back.

I heard a dresser drawer close then Brian cleared his throat. "Olivia, you didn't have anything to do with this guy's death, did you?"

"I swear, no! I confronted him this morning and told him we were not going to be blackmailed by him anymore and he'd better not send anything to us again or else there would be consequences. That's it. I promise."

I scrunched my nose when I heard kissing noises.

Time to move this party along.

I waved Aunt Shirley on to where we were supposed to be going—the Harley Quin room where Stewart and Tina Collins were staying.

I knocked on the door and waited a few seconds. When no one answered, I knocked again.

"What?" Stewart Collins shouted. "I'm busy here. Come back later."

"Mr. Collins?" I said as I knocked on the door again. No way was I leaving this jerk alone. He'd have to answer the door and physically tell me to stop. Which would allow us to ask questions real quick.

"What?" Stewart Collins yanked open the door and glared at me. "Didn't you hear me tell you to go away?"

I gave him my most innocent look. "No. I'm sorry, I didn't hear you. My aunt and I would like to ask you a couple questions, if you don't mind."

"I do mind."

He went to shut the door in my face, so I stuck my foot in the door frame. He glared at me, then moved his glare over to Aunt Shirley.

"We just had a couple questions about the death of Trent Starnes," I said.

"I already talked to the Sheriff. I don't need to talk to you. I had no idea who this Trent guy even was."

"What about your wife?" Aunt Shirley prompted. "What did she tell the Sheriff about Trent?"

Stewart Collins gave me a funny look. "My wife? She didn't know him either. I think she told the Sheriff she may have spoken to him when she was here previously. But she said she hadn't spoken to him at all since we've been here the last two days."

Well, in her defense, they weren't doing a whole lot of talking!

"Ya know, Stewart," Aunt Shirley said, "you're a huge jerk. And you probably deserve what's coming your way, but I'm here to tell you right now your wife knew Trent a little bit more than she's let on."

Anger clouded Stewart's face. "And you're a meddling old fool. Do not presume to tell me who my wife may or may not know. Now, I don't think we have anything more to talk about."

He slammed the door in my face.

I turned to Aunt Shirley. "I'm not even sure how to read that relationship. Or really who I feel sorrier for. I just hope to high heaven they don't ever have kids."

We started back to our room when Stewart's door opened again. I turned and saw a distraught Tina standing in the hallway. She looked over her shoulder back into the bedroom before motioning us over.

"What did you tell Stewart?" Tina asked.

I shrugged my shoulders. "We just asked him a couple questions."

Tina chewed on her lower lip. "Did you say anything about seeing me in the barn? Because I can explain. I went in there to set up an appointment with Trent to go horseback riding. That's all."

Aunt Shirley and I both snorted.

"It's true!" Tina cried as she narrowed her eyes at us.

"Try playing that song and dance somewhere else, girlie," Aunt Shirley said. "We know the truth."

Anger flashed in Tina's eyes. "You don't know jack, old lady. I already told the Sheriff and my husband the truth. You have no proof otherwise."

I chuckled. "I wouldn't exactly say that, Tina."

Tina paled. "What do you mean?" She grabbed hold of my arm, her nails digging into me.

"She means we saw you and Trent doing the horizontal hula…bumpin' uglies…knockin' boots…playing a little hide the sal—"

"Okay," I laughed. "I think she gets the picture."

Tina dropped my arm, ran back into her room, and slammed the door shut. Aunt Shirley and I shrugged at each other and went back to our rooms to put the pieces of the puzzle together.

I knew I had to call Garrett soon and let him know what happened. At the pace we were going, I'm not sure we could solve this crime and be on the road by tomorrow like we'd planned.

"I'm gonna take a bath," Aunt Shirley announced. "Let my body soak and my brain think."

I laughed. "You do that."

Deciding it was now or never, I picked up my cell phone and punched in Garrett's number. Just my luck he answered on the second ring.

"Hey, Sin. What's up? I miss you."

I steadied my breath. "Not a whole lot. It's fun here."

"Fun? Okay, what's happened?"

I sighed. "What makes you think something has happened?"

Garrett chuckled. "Because I heard the hitch in your breath, and never would you describe an outing where you have to sleep with your aunt as fun. So, again, what's happened?"

"I found a dead body."

Silence.

"Sin, honey, aren't you *supposed* to find a dead body…maybe even two?"

I laughed shakily. "Yes, but usually they are props. I mean I found an actual dead body."

Garrett sighed. "Of course you did. Because you wouldn't be the woman I've come to love if things actually went according to plan."

My stomach pitched. Hearing his declaration of love always warmed me…but did he have to say it like loving me was a burden or a cross to bear?

"Why don't you fill me in?" Garrett interrupted my thoughts.

So I filled him in on everything. From the moment we got to Mystery Farms until our latest encounter with Tina and having the door slammed in my face.

Garrett chuckled. "Who knew Aunt Shirley knew that many euphemisms for sex?"

"You're disgusting!" I laughed.

"Guilty. And this Lester Simpson character is *really* a Sheriff?" Garrett asked. "Maybe I'll give him a call and see what's going on."

I sighed. "You mean you'll call him and ask him what the heck he was thinking asking Aunt Shirley and me to help in a homicide investigation."

"Guilty again. I mean, really, what was he thinking?"

"We are only supposed to be asking the people around here questions. We aren't supposed to be investigating or deciphering clues. But then Aunt Shirley assured him that we had single-handedly solved three or four cases already."

Garrett sucked in his breath. "You're telling me she's going around touting herself as a detective?"

Oops. Gonna have to talk him off the ledge now.

"No. She just told Sheriff Simpson we had been in many situations where we had to solve crimes. Mainly after we'd been kidnapped, poisoned, and nearly killed. But it impressed Sheriff Simpson enough he asked us *only* to listen in on what's going on. See if anyone would talk with us. Harmless, really."

Garrett groaned. "Until the killer decides you're asking too many questions and you need to be dealt with."

Well, yeah, there's that.

"I hate sounding like a harpy," Garrett growled, "but would it really be too much to ask for you to go one month without stumbling over a dead body?"

I giggled at the thought of Garrett being a harpy.

He finally chuckled. "Hush up. I'm serious. I love you so much, that the thought of something bad happening to you puts me in a lecturing mood."

Lecture away!

"Do you want me to come down and help out? If this Sheriff Simpson is as strapped as you say, perhaps he wouldn't mind help from another *actual* police officer."

I paused. I personally wouldn't mind the help—and the backup weapons. But I knew Aunt Shirley would be devastated if she thought someone was honing in on her territory.

"No. I think we have everything under control here. Like I said, Sheriff Simpson just wanted us to talk to the guests and employees here. Only because he thought they'd open up to us. I don't think we've done anything that would cause Aunt Shirley or me any harm."

"Hmm. I'm not so sure. But I trust you. Just know I'm here if you need any help."

My pulse raced at his words. He was actually going to let us help out with an investigation without a huge lecture! "I will. I promise. And I also promise not to do anything too crazy."

"It's not you I worry about…it's that crazy aunt of yours!"

I hung up while things were on a positive note. Sometimes Aunt Shirley had a tendency to sour good spirits.

Next I called Hank to check in with him.

"How are all the little Nancy Drews doing?" Hank asked snidely around the unlit cigar in his mouth.

I rolled my eyes. "We're fine. Listen, before you start drilling me too much, just know I haven't solved anything yet, but when I do, you'll get the exclusive."

Hank barked out a laugh. "The newspaper ain't that hard up I need you writing about a pretend murder you and your aunt solved."

I smiled, knowing I had him. "Oh, did I imply it was *fake?*" I laughed when I heard his chair squeaking in the background. That obviously got his attention enough he decided to sit up and take notice.

"Spill it, Sinclair. Whaddya got for me?"

I paused and relished in the glory of having one-upped Hank. It was rare I could do it. I heard him growl and knew I'd kept him waiting long enough.

"Mystery Farms didn't just supply us with a fake murder, but they also supplied us with a real murder."

Just like with Garrett, I went on to tell him everything I knew so far. When I was finished, he whistled.

"So you and Aunt Shirley are actually helping out with the case? Is that wise?"

Okay, Garrett junior!

"Yes, it's wise. Hopefully we'll have the murderer identified and apprehended by tomorrow."

"Front-page story for you if you do," Hank promised.

I let out a little squeal of delight. "Tell Mindy hi for me. Talk to you soon."

I hung up as Aunt Shirley walked out of the bathroom wrapped in a bathrobe. "I've been thinking, and darned if I'm not mad at myself for not thinking of it before. I know the post office is probably closed by now, but we need to get to the post office in Millsap and see if the post master knows anything. Legally he can't tell us who rented the box, but I don't think the law says anything about nodding yes or no when it comes to describing someone."

I looked at Aunt Shirley in astonishment. That actually *was* a great idea. "Maybe Mr. Wainwright will know something. As a business owner he must know a lot of people. Want me to run down to his office and see if he can help us out?" I asked.

"Do I really need to answer that question for you?"

I rolled my eyes at Aunt Shirley's sarcasm. "Fine. I'll be back in a second. It will give me a chance to return Trent's key without getting caught, too."

I strolled down the stairs and said a quick prayer of thanks that no one was behind the counter. I quickly slipped the extra key on the hook and then made my way to Gary Wainwright's office. His door was closed but I could hear muted sounds within. I knocked and he opened the door immediately.

"Ryli, good to see you. Come in."

Cybil was sitting at her desk writing. She actually looked better than I'd seen her look all weekend. Guess having your husband believe you aren't cheating helps with the nerves.

"Mr. Wainwright, Aunt Shirley and I have come across something, and we're hoping you can help us out."

"Of course. I'll do what I can."

"All the envelopes have the same address as to where to send the money. I'm wondering…"

"All?" Cybil exclaimed and threw down her pen. "There are others?"

I winced. I totally forgot the Wainwrights knew nothing of Olivia's horrific ordeal. "Yes. I'm afraid there have been others here at the farm who have been blackmailed by Trent."

Gary gasped. "Who?"

"Olivia Banner for one."

"No!" Cybil cried. "Is that why her husband didn't come with her?"

Gary's brow furrowed. "But he is here. I just checked him in a little while ago. I admit Olivia seemed shocked at seeing him, but I thought that was just because he surprised her."

"It seems Trent not only sent Olivia blackmail pictures of them together, but even after she paid him, he then sent them to her husband."

Cybil Wainwright put her hands over her face and started to weep. My heart broke for her. I really liked these people, and they certainly didn't deserve this kind of torment.

Gary Wainwright rushed over to where his wife was sitting. His red face and tic in his jaw left no doubt he was angry. "I wonder how many more people that have stayed at our place have been blackmailed by that little—"

A knock on the door interrupted Gary.

CHAPTER 11

"Aunt Cybil, Uncle Gary, what's going on?" Dayna Bowers stood in the doorway, wringing her hands in worry. "Is it about Trent?"

Gary motioned for Dayna to come in. "Yes. It seems Trent has been carrying on with visitors here and then blackmailing them with pictures he would take. He would send the pictures to the women and then to their husbands."

Dayna put her hands on her stomach and bent over. "I think I'm going to be sick."

I walked over to where she was standing and gently eased her down on a nearby chair. "I'm so sorry about this, Dayna."

"Who?" Dayna demanded. "Who else is being blackmailed?"

I hesitated. I definitely didn't want to get into family disputes, but I figured they had a right to know. After all, it was their business that will probably suffer from this backlash.

I took a deep breath. "Olivia Banner."

Dayna reeled back in her chair as though I'd slapped her. "Olivia? But her husband just arrived. I went up to see if she needed extra towels just a few minutes ago, and they didn't look like…" Dayna's face turned red. "I mean, they didn't look to be having any problems."

I smiled. "That's a new development. It seems her husband, Brian, came here to beg her to forgive him and together they were going to set Trent straight."

Gary Wainwright gave me a hard look. "You don't think maybe Olivia's husband had anything to do with Trent's murder, do you?"

"I honestly don't. He has a pretty solid alibi. It seems he was at Olivia's mom's house begging to know where Olivia was. He only found out where she was this morning when he drove straight here. Of course, that's their story. Sheriff Simpson would have to go through more in-depth questioning to find out if it's true or not."

Gary sighed. "So we are no closer to solving this crime." He sat down behind his desk. "You said others. Do you know of anyone else that Trent was scamming?"

I looked at Dayna. I wasn't sure the girl should be hearing this. After all, she was supposedly seeing Trent.

"It's okay," Dayna assured me. "I've come to terms with the fact Trent was a scumbag."

I hid my smile. "Well, I don't know if he has sent anything before, but I know Tina—"

Dayna snorted. "I *knew* it! Trent kept saying I was being paranoid, but I knew he was fooling around with her!"

I bit my lip. "Yes. Like I said, I'm not sure about before, but I'm afraid Aunt Shirley and I came across some pretty incriminating evidence that we will turn over to Sheriff Simpson when we see him next. But when we questioned Stewart, he didn't seem to believe what Aunt Shirley and I were telling him. And short of showing him the sordid video, he probably never will. Or he will believe us, but just not care."

"That's probably more like it," Cybil said. "Tina usually comes here with a group of girls. This is the first time we've ever met Stewart. I see now why she doesn't bring him places."

"Do you think…" Dayna bit her lip and looked away. "Do you think Tina brought Stewart here to rub it in his face that she was messing around?"

I frowned. "Maybe. I guess anything's possible. But I don't know how that fits in with the murder."

Cybil clapped her hands together. "Maybe this is all a show for Stewart and he really does care. Maybe Trent sent Stewart blackmail photos and Stewart came here to kill Trent."

I slowly nodded my head. "Yes. But that's a lot of maybes. And it's a pretty elaborate show if you ask me. I honestly don't think Stewart cares one way or the other."

We all collectively sighed. It was like we were spinning in circles and had nowhere else to go.

"What did you want to ask me about the post office?" Gary said.

"Oh, yeah," I said. "Do you know the post master over at Millsap? I know they can't tell us who owns the box, or give out any personal information. But maybe they could describe the person for us without realizing it."

Gary Wainwright shrugged. "Worth a shot. The post master's name is Larry Tubbins. He's a good guy. I'll give him a call and see what he can tell me. Hopefully I'll have something for you by dinner tonight."

I thanked him and went back upstairs to let Aunt Shirley know what I'd found out. I closed the door and walked in on her standing in her bathrobe by the open window smoking her e-cig.

I rolled my eyes. "Will you never grow up? Put that stupid thing away."

"Fine," she grumbled as she threw it back in her open makeup bag. She reached down into her bathrobe pocket and pulled out a flask. She opened the lid, took a sip, and grinned at me. "Better?"

I rolled my eyes and refused to answer. "I'm going to take a bath. Mr. Wainwright said he knew the post master and he would give him a call. Hopefully he'll have something for us at dinner tonight."

I gathered up clean clothes and went to the bathroom to take a soothing bubble bath. I poured in my fragrance, turned on my music app, sank down into the tub, and closed my eyes.

Pounding on the door caused me to groan. I wasn't sure how long I'd been in the tub, but the cool water let me know it had been awhile.

"What?" I yelled.

"You're gonna be a prune. Get out of there. We have about thirty minutes before supper. Shake a leg."

I knew Aunt Shirley was right, but I just couldn't bring myself to get out and get ready. I drained some of the water then refilled it with fresh, piping hot water. I needed a few more minutes.

More pounding. "Are you forgetting we can have cocktails before dinner? I'm sure everyone is downstairs already getting their drink on while you're in here lollygagging."

I sighed and unplugged the water. It was going to take me ten minutes—tops—to get ready. Put on some lotion, slip on my maxi dress, brush out my hair and pull it back up in a knot, and maybe throw on some mascara.

"I'm coming," I yelled through the door. "I'll be out in a few minutes and we can go."

I heard grumbling, but the answer must have sufficed because I didn't hear anything else out of her. I slipped on my dress and finished getting ready.

"About time," Aunt Shirley whined when I came out of the bathroom. "I'm wasting away. I need food and drink. And not necessarily in that order."

I bit back a laugh and stuck my cell phone in my dress pocket. "Let's go then."

By the time we made it to the parlor, the only people missing were Stewart and Tina. Wayne Skaggs already had Mom and Paige cornered, talking their ear off. He had on the same suit as this morning, but he did change out the colored handkerchief. It was now a deep purple.

Olivia and Brian were canoodling on the couch, Dayna was busy serving drinks, and Gary and Cybil were talking with Sheriff Simpson.

I turned to Aunt Shirley. "Did you bring the camcorder for Sheriff Simpson?"

Aunt Shirley tapped her oversize purse. "Got it in here. I'll take care of that business—alone." Aunt Shirley waggled her brows at me.

Yuck!

"Fine. I'm going over to rescue Mom and Paige from Wayne. You go talk with Sheriff Simpson."

I sauntered over to the fireplace where Mom and Paige were standing. I could tell by the look on Mom's face she was about out of patience with Wayne. Which explained the champagne. Mom wasn't much of a drinker, but tonight she was having a glass of champagne.

"Ah, Ryli, don't you look lovely," Wayne said as I joined them. "I was just telling your mom how stunning she looked tonight. It's easy to see where you get it from."

I snorted. While Mom's beauty was effortless, she never flaunted it. Tonight she had her hair pulled back in a French braid, a simple button-up top, and slacks. No makeup, no fuss. That was my mom.

"Yes. She is a gem. Her boyfriend, *Doctor* Powell, is always saying so." I thought the added emphasis on the doctor would help Wayne see he didn't stand a chance. Of course, now I went and made it awkward for everyone.

Dayna entered the parlor again. "Bessie said dinner will be ready in about five minutes. If you'd finish up your drinks, we can retire to the dining room."

"Excuse me, ladies," Wayne said. "I think I'll get a quick refill before dinner."

We all watched him walk away. I yelped when I felt a pinch on my arm.

"What?" I said. Even though I knew what Mom was gonna say. Paige was already giggling.

"Did you have to emphasize the doctor?" Mom asked.

I nodded my head. "Yes, I did. I don't think the guy is gonna take the hint otherwise."

Mom sighed. "You may be right. He asked to take me for a walk after dinner. I don't know how to dodge the man."

"I may know of a way," Aunt Shirley said as she came up behind us. We shifted to include her in our group.

"What's up?" I asked.

"First off," Aunt Shirley said looking at Paige. "How's my niece doing in there?" She gave Paige a little pat on her still-flat stomach.

I laughed at Paige's face. "Yes, let that sink in. Aunt Shirley is going to want to play with your baby. Teach her all sorts of things. How to break into other people's houses, how to shave her head and dye it purple, how to drink from a flask instead of a baby bottle."

Paige blanched and grabbed hold of her flat belly as if protecting the child. "I don't think so."

Aunt Shirley shrugged and took a gulp of her homemade margarita. "Don't sound all that bad to me. She's gonna need to know these things in order to survive."

Mom took pity on Paige and steered the conversation in another direction. "You said you may know of a way to keep Wayne from me tonight. What did you mean by that?"

"Well, after I gave Sheriff Simpson the camcorder, I asked Gary if he'd heard anything more from the post master. And he said that the post master, Larry Tubbins, would talk with us tonight."

"Wow, really?" I asked. "Like at his house?"

Aunt Shirley grinned. "Nope. Like at a bar. I guess tonight there's a big competition over at the Lazy J Saloon in Millsap, and

Ole Larry isn't willing to miss it. But, if we go to him, he'll talk with us."

Paige groaned. "I don't see anything good coming from this."

I couldn't agree more.

I looked around the room but didn't see Sheriff Simpson. "Where did the Sheriff go?"

"He wanted to take a look at the footage I gave him. Plus, he said he was waiting for a call from the coroner and the one deputy that was on call tonight needed relieved."

"But we aren't supposed to leave the house," Paige reminded Aunt Shirley.

Aunt Shirley grinned. "I told Sheriff Simpson that you girls were surprising me with a night out on the town for my birthday. When I pouted about not being able to leave the farm, he said he didn't see what a couple hours out could hurt."

She is good.

"I think I'll pass," Mom said.

"Pass on what?" Wayne asked as he joined our group again. "I hope it's not on our moonlight walk tonight."

Mom sighed. "Yes. I was telling the girls I'd have to pass on your offer because I need to go somewhere with them later on."

Wayne frowned. "You're going out after dinner? I thought Sheriff Simpson said we weren't allowed to leave?"

I thought fast. "We aren't, but he gave us special permission to go somewhere for Aunt Shirley's birthday."

"And I have some information I want to check out," Aunt Shirley boasted.

"What kind of information?" Wayne asked. "Do you have a lead or something?"

There was no way I wanted to tell this man anything. While he wasn't even a blip on my radar as a suspect, I didn't think we could trust him. Wayne seemed to be all about Wayne.

"Not exactly a lead," Aunt Shirley said vaguely. "More of we have a question that needs answered. Nothing too promising, yet."

"Do you need me to go with you?" Wayne asked. "Sometimes having a man around—"

"Is a drag," Aunt Shirley finished.

Wayne's frown turned into a full scowl. "I only meant you might need protecting, and I was offering my services."

Mom held up her champagne glass as though she were holding court. "Thank you all the same, Wayne, but we will be fine. There's not a single woman here who can't shoot her way out of trouble."

That shut him up.

"Dinner is ready," Dayna announced as she walked into the room.

"Thank goodness," Aunt Shirley said as she knocked back the last of her drink.

I couldn't agree more.

CHAPTER 12

"How many changes of clothes did you bring?" I asked as I watched Aunt Shirley rifle through her side of the dresser.

"I came prepared," Aunt Shirley said without lifting her head.

"I don't understand why you need to change. You look fine."

She actually looked normal for once. She'd worn a pair of slacks and flowered button-down shirt to dinner. Now that we were about to head to the Lazy J Saloon, she wanted to change. We told Mom and Paige we'd go to their door instead of meeting in the parlor. I think Mom wanted to stay clear of an accidental run-in with Wayne.

"Where is it?" Aunt Shirley muttered.

Please don't let it be from the same store she bought the riding outfit from. Please, no. Please, no.

"Here it is!" Aunt Shirley yanked out a forest green dress with white fringe running from her shoulders down to a V under her chest. There was also white fringe running around the bottom hem.

"What is it with you and your sudden fascination with fringe and tassels?" I asked.

"It's the latest craze," Aunt Shirley informed me snootily.

I laughed. "So is the male romper. But you don't see me begging Garrett to wear one, do you?"

Aunt Shirley snorted. "That would be pretty funny, though." She held the dress in front of her and swayed, causing the fringe to move. "I think it's perfect."

I held in a sigh and said nothing. I learned a long time ago not to mess with Aunt Shirley when she had her mind made up.

I went into the bathroom to put on some makeup while she got dressed. I reached in my dress, pulled out my cell phone, and called Garrett.

"This is Kimble."

"This is Sinclair. What's up?"

Garrett chuckled. "Sorry, Sin. I didn't even look at the screen. I'm over at Matt's with Doc Powell, watching the ballgame tonight."

"Three men, alone, without wives or girlfriends in town on a Saturday night and you all are watching a ballgame on TV? Wow, Kimble, you really know how to live it up."

Garrett lowered his voice. "It's a good thing I like that smart mouth of your, Sin."

The low rumble of his voice caused my stomach to flutter. I missed him, so much. And that scared me. When I thought about spending the rest of my life with him, it left me breathless. When I thought about what comes after that…the spit in my mouth dried up. I was eager for the commitment, scared of the future.

"You still there, Sin?"

I shook myself. "Yep. Just checking in seeing what you were up to. Mom, Paige, Aunt Shirley, and I are going to a bar called the Lazy J Saloon tonight."

Garrett chuckled. "I really can't see your mom in a place like that."

I laughed. "Yeah, well, don't tell Doc, but there's some guy here that keeps hitting on Mom. So in order to avoid him she's going with us."

Garrett growled. "Is this guy bad news?"

I snorted. "No. He's an actor who fancies himself an author. But now that we aren't doing the murder mystery, he's really more of a nuisance."

"Speaking of the murder. I didn't think you guys were supposed to leave the farm? Wasn't that Sheriff Simpson's orders?"

I sighed. "Yes. But Aunt Shirley had an idea about something we stumbled across today. So she somehow convinced Sheriff Simpson to let us out for a few hours under the guise that we are celebrating Aunt Shirley's birthday tonight."

I could tell by the huge intake of breath he was going to remind me of my role—a reporter, not a detective. "Oh, Ryli. What am I going to do with you?"

Love me. Marry me. Have babies with me. Eek! Where had that last part come from?

"Please be careful," Garrett said, interrupting my crazy thoughts. "Keep me posted. The game just started so we'll be up late. Let me know how things go."

"You bet."

I hung up and walked out into the bedroom area. Aunt Shirley was on the bed putting on her shoes. They were typical "old lady" shoes. White patent leather strappy sandals with a one-inch heel. Cushiony on the inside, and slippery as heck on the bottom. There's no way she was going to be able to run in those if we needed to run. And with Aunt Shirley, usually we needed to run.

"Hope we don't need to outrun anyone tonight," I said, hoping she'd take the hint.

"I don't have boots. I should probably invest in boots now that I have this dress. Maybe I can get Old Man Jenkins to take me to a honky-tonk in Brywood when I get back."

I laughed at the thought of ninety-year-old Mr. Jenkins line dancing at a bar. Although, he was nuts about Aunt Shirley, so I'm sure if she asked, he'd go.

Aunt Shirley picked up her oversized patent leather pink purse and headed toward the door. I bit my tongue to keep from laughing. A forest green cowgirl dress, white dress shoes, a bright pink purse, and purple hair on one side of her head. You couldn't miss Aunt Shirley if you tried.

Mom and Paige were waiting for us in the hallway. They were talking with Olivia and Brian Banner. Even though I was happy to see the Banners had made up, I couldn't help but wonder if it was all an act. Two scenarios ran through my head for the Banners.

Either Brian was lying about his alibi and he already knew where his wife was going, drove down early this morning, and waited for an opportune time to kill Trent. Then waited and surprised her with his confession to make up.

Or scenario two was that they were in it together. Olivia came down under the pretense that her and her husband had split, but in actuality, they planned on murdering Trent the whole time. Their convenient make-up session was just a ruse on getting away with murder.

So while they weren't at the top on my list of suspects, they were definitely still there. I was still leaning toward Stewart Collins, one of the Wainwrights, Bessie, or Dayna. If I had to pick—I was hoping for Stewart.

"Have a good night," Mom said to the Banners as we made our way down the hall.

"We will," Olivia said.

The four of us tiptoed down the stairs. We didn't want to draw attention to ourselves. We hopped in the Falcon and Paige pulled up her navigation app. She plugged in the coordinates, and I pointed the Falcon toward Millsap. It was nice to get out of the house for a while.

It only took about twenty minutes to get to Millsap. The Lazy J Saloon was located on the outskirts of town about three miles. I pulled onto a gravel road and slowed the Falcon down. No sense ruining the paint job. After about two miles I saw lights.

When the Lazy J finally came into view, my first thought was it was more of a shed than an actual building. A really *big* shed…but still a shed. The parking lot was only half full. Of course, it was still considered early by bar-hopping standards.

I parked the Falcon and we carefully made our way to the Lazy J Saloon. A big burly bouncer stopped us at the door to check our IDs. I dug into my purse and handed him my license.

"Next?" he motioned with his hands.

I turned to look at Aunt Shirley. "Give him your license so we can get through."

Aunt Shirley made a face. "I don't have it on me."

"Look lady," Big Bad Bouncer said as he slowly scanned her from head to toe and took in her crazy outfit, "no one gets in without proper ID." He leaned over and looked around Aunt Shirley to make sure no one else was standing there. The movement cause his shirt to ride up on his arms. I could make out the bottom half of a USMC tattoo.

While one part of me understood his need to follow the rules, the other part of me wanted to shout at him that *obviously* he could see that Aunt Shirley was older than Methuselah and that made her well over twenty-one. Heck, anyone with eyes could see she was well over seventy-one.

Aunt Shirley must have seen the tattoo also, because she got that look on her face that said, "We are kindred spirits." She reached over and patted Big Bad Bouncer on his shoulder.

He looked at his shoulder then scowled down at Aunt Shirley. She was not intimidated. "Marine, let me tell you why I didn't bring my ID with me this evening. I knew we would be doing reconnaissance work tonight. And if things went south, I didn't want my name known."

Big Bad Bouncer stared at Aunt Shirley, then slowly one corner of his mouth lifted and he let out a little chuckle. "Is that right, Ma'am?"

"Yes, sir. Me and my girls here are on a mission to find *a murderer*. And we've been given special permission by Sheriff Simpson to ferret out this bad guy and take him down. There's a gentleman in this here saloon that may have the information we need to make this takedown possible. But if things go bad—and I will admit, past history shows that sometimes they do—I don't want to be easily identified."

By the time Aunt Shirley finished her ridiculous speech, Big Bad Bouncer was wearing a full-on grin. He must have liked what he heard, because he nodded his head. "Makes sense." He looked over his shoulder then back at Aunt Shirley. "Okay. This one time I'll let you in. But only because it's been a long time since I've been involved with a recon mission, and something tells me I'd like to see you in action."

Aunt Shirley grinned. "You wait and see. By the time I come back out tonight, I'll have the answers I need."

Big Bad Bouncer shook his head but lifted his arm to signal us in. We hurried around him and made our way inside before he changed his mind.

CHAPTER 13

It took a few seconds for my eyes to adjust to the darkness of the room. The only real light was by the actual bar and the glow of neon lights from signs plastered around the room. Directly in front of us was a large dance floor that took up most of the space in the shed. There were approximately fifteen people jammed around the bar located on the left side of the shed, six people playing pool in the back-left corner, a handful more watching them or just talking with each other, and maybe ten people on the dance floor line dancing. Toward the back of the shed on the right, a couple people were already riding a mechanical bull. The music was loud enough it almost bordered on annoying.

"Let's grab a table near the dance floor," Aunt Shirley shouted. "That looks to be the best place to observe."

Mom grabbed me by the arm and pulled me to her. Aunt Shirley and Paige kept walking toward an empty table near the dance floor. "I heard Aunt Shirley tell that man that past experiences has you two with a lot of failures and you guys running. Do I want to know what that's about?"

I hesitated for only a minute. "You know how over-the-top Aunt Shirley can be. It's not as bad as she makes it out to be."

It's worse.

Mom slowly closed her eyes. I wasn't sure if she was praying or not…but if she knew the disasters Aunt Shirley and I usually got tangled up in, she'd definitely be praying.

Mom finally opened her eyes. "Lead on. This should be an interesting night."

I grinned at her. "Yeah. I mean, you could be at the farm trying to avoid Wayne. Instead, you're here with us girls ready to sniff out some clues and capture a murderer."

Mom frowned but said nothing more as we caught up to where Aunt Shirley and Paige were already sitting waiting on us. Aunt Shirley clapped her hands together. "Let's order drinks."

"Do you really think that's a good idea?" Mom asked. "Aren't we here to ask a man a couple questions? How can you drink and do that at the same time?"

Aunt Shirley snorted. "Sometimes when you talk, Janine, it's like my sister is still right here in front of me."

I stiffened. Rarely does Aunt Shirley talk about her sister—my mom's mom and my grandma. The only thing my mom ever said about the relationship between grandma and Aunt Shirley was that Aunt Shirley had always been a wild child and ran away to California in the early sixties.

My grandma was the complete opposite of Aunt Shirley. She married my grandpa right out of high school. She was always a stay-at-home mom. She could cook like a professional chef—which is where my mom got it from—and she was always kind and sweet. And, most importantly, she was a teetotaler.

"I'll take a water," Paige said, trying to diffuse the suddenly tense situation.

"And I'll take a white wine," Mom said tightly.

I suddenly panicked. I didn't know what to do. Usually I blindly follow Aunt Shirley's lead, but with Mom in the picture, I didn't want her to see how easily manipulated I was by Aunt

Shirley. Because the truth was, as much as I complained about Aunt Shirley, I liked hanging out with her and getting in trouble with her.

Mom must have seen the battle going on inside me. She laid her hand on my arm. "Order whatever you want. You two know how to do this interrogation stuff more than I do."

I grinned. "Gin and Tonic."

Aunt Shirley smiled appreciatively at me. "The ole Gin Rickey. Nice choice."

One thing I'd learned from the crazy neighbors of Aunt Shirley's a couple months ago…how to drink like a woman. Lovey, Dotty, and Virginia instilled in me an appreciation for traditional cocktails.

Aunt Shirley walked toward the bar and flagged down a jeans and plaid-shirt wearing waitress and gave her our orders. The waitress then pointed to a guy that was drinking at the bar.

"Larry's here and at the bar drinking," Aunt Shirley said when she came back. "I figure we have our drinks and let him get down in his cups a little more before we go question him."

A few minutes later the waitress came by with our drinks. We sipped silently and watched the dancers on the floor. By the time we finished our drinks, and watched the dancers some more, a good thirty minutes had passed.

Aunt Shirley looked over at the bar. Larry looked to be having a good time. "I say we strike now." She finished off the last of her margarita and stood up. "We'll go to him."

Mom held up her hand. "I think I'm fine staying right here and watching the dancers. Paige, if you want to go, that's fine. I'll watch our purses."

Paige looked at me gave me a half smile. "Actually, if you don't mind, I think I'll wait here, too. I'm starting to get awful tired."

Aunt Shirley nodded. "We'll be back soon. I don't foresee this taking too long."

We made our way through the crowd of people who were now milling around. In the half hour we'd sipped our drinks and bided our time, the saloon had pretty much filled to capacity.

I gauged Larry Tubbins to be in his fifties or sixties. It was hard to tell with the big cowboy hat on top of his head. He was a little on the short side but had a solid build on him—if you didn't count the massive beer gut he was sporting.

Aunt Shirley and I pushed through the last of the patrons to stand next to Larry. He looked over at Aunt Shirley and did a double take.

"Well, hello there, doll face. Don't believe I've seen you around these parts."

I rolled my eyes and knew we were in trouble. Mainly because I knew what a sucker Aunt Shirley was for these lame one-liners men threw her way.

Aunt Shirley shimmied a little so her fringe flew. "My niece and I are here on vacation. We have a mutual friend, Gary Wainwright."

Larry's face split into a grin. "Then it's my lucky night. You're here to see me."

Aunt Shirley stuck out her hand. "You can call me Twila, and this is my niece, Ryli."

I snorted. I was fairly certain Gary Wainwright had told Larry who he'd be meeting, but Larry must've had too many drinks to realize Twila was a made-up name.

"Twila." Larry slurred a little as he turned to face Aunt Shirley fully. "Now that right there is a mighty purdy name for a mighty purdy lady. Can I buy you a drink?"

"Actually," I interrupted before Aunt Shirley could agree, "we just need to ask you some quick questions."

Larry Tubbins smiled. "Little lady, around these parts, nothing is done quickly." He gave Aunt Shirley a lewd wink.

I groaned when Aunt Shirley tittered and batted her eyes at Larry.

"So here's my proposal," Larry went on drunkenly. "As you know, I can't give you any personal information. But maybe if you ask the right questions I may give you something that can help you. Here's the catch—you want to ask a question, it will cost you a shot."

"We have to buy you a shot for every question we ask you?" I asked incredulously.

"Nope. Twila here has to take a shot with me for every question you two ask me."

Aunt Shirley grinned. "Deal."

If I'd been standing at the bar I would have plunked my head down on the counter. This wasn't going to be good.

Larry threw his hand up in the air to signal the bartender. "What's your shot of choice?"

Aunt Shirley didn't even hesitate. "Tequila."

Larry grinned. "You ain't married are ya?"

Aunt Shirley laughed. "Not yet."

I turned around and looked at our table. Paige and Mom were whispering and staring at us. I sent them a pleading look for help, but Mom just smiled and shook her head. I turned back around as the bartender finished pouring each of them a shot.

Aunt Shirley reached over and selected three limes from the white compartmentalized container sitting in front of her. She placed the limes on her napkin and then grabbed the salt shaker.

"I want to know about a box in your post office," Aunt Shirley said.

"Drink," Larry commanded. Aunt Shirley picked up the salt shaker and shook salt on one of the limes. They both took the shot. Aunt Shirley bit into the lime and smiled at Larry.

"Okay," Larry said happily. "That's one question."

I frowned. "That wasn't exactly a question."

Larry grinned drunkenly at me. "It is if I say it is." He motioned the bartender to pour them another. "What do you want to know?"

The bartender backed away and Aunt Shirley and Larry picked up the shot glasses and toasted. I noticed Aunt Shirley didn't even bother with the salt and lime this time. "I want to know what you can tell me about the person that rents the box."

They both threw back the drinks, shook their heads and let out a yell. Larry banged his fist on the counter. "You can hold your booze there, little lady."

Aunt Shirley grinned. "Years of practice."

Larry grunted. "Gary said y'all were working with Sheriff Simpson on this case. Here's the thing, I can't give you precise information. Gary did give me the box number, so I'm familiar with the box you're talking about."

I motioned to him with my hands. "And?"

Larry's brow furrowed in thought. "And I can tell you I've never personally seen the person that comes and gets the mail out of the box. They probably sneak in during the night to come get it. As long as you have a box, you have a key to get in the building. So they probably come in when no one else is around. If we had cameras, I'd say it would be an easy thing of Sheriff Simpson getting a warrant, but we don't have cameras."

My heart sank. This wasn't what I wanted to hear. I wanted to hear that Trent Starnes came in and opened the box and he was the one that collected the mail.

Larry signaled the bartender for another round. Why I didn't know. We had no more need of Larry Tubbins.

"But…" Larry grinned wickedly.

Aunt Shirley put some salt on a different lime. "But you remember something that may help us?"

Larry held up his shot of tequila and clinked it with Aunt Shirley's glass. "Twila, you are not only beautiful, but smart."

They grinned at each other and took their shot. Aunt Shirley bit into the lime and grimaced. She'd better not get sick in the Falcon or I'd make her walk. Of course, I'd seen Aunt Shirley toss back way more tequila than she was now, but you never know how things will go with Aunt Shirley.

Larry wiped his mouth with the back of his hand and let out a loud belch.

Classy.

"See, I was the person that opened the account for the box."

I leaned in close. "And?"

He looked at me and swayed a little on his feet. His skin was pale and sweaty underneath the ruddy red from his cheeks. I had no idea how he was getting home that night, but he was going to need that ride soon. Larry didn't break eye contact with me but threw up his hand to signal the bartender.

"One more," he yelled drunkenly before turning around.

Aunt Shirley looked at me and rolled her eyes. She was still sober as a nun and this all was just a game for her.

She painstakingly put salt on the last of her lime as the bartender shook his head. I couldn't help but wonder what this little interrogation was going to cost us. Those shots were probably six or seven dollars apiece. I calculated the total in my head and groaned.

Larry held up his glass. "Before I tell you what the person looked like that opened the box at the post office, I'll make a little wager with you."

Aunt Shirley narrowed her eyes. "I'm listening."

"I'll give you a full description of the person *and* pay for all these drinks if…" Larry trailed off and leaned closer to Aunt Shirley, "you ride the mechanical bull over there."

"No," I said. "No way. You will break a hip."

Aunt Shirley scowled at me. "It's my body…my decision."

Okay…different approach.

"You're in a dress," I said. "Aren't you the one that said you can't straddle a horse in a dress that it would be tacky?"

"Yep," Aunt Shirley agreed. "Good thing it's a bull and not a horse."

I threw my hands up in the air. "That makes absolutely no sense!"

Ignoring me, Aunt Shirley looked over at Larry, assessing him. "Let me get this straight. You will pay for all these drinks and give me a description of the person that opened the box, and all I have to do is take a ride on the mechanical bull?"

"Yep."

Aunt Shirley's face lit up. "Whoop! Let's ride!"

CHAPTER 14

I ran back to where Mom and Paige were sitting. No way was I letting Aunt Shirley get up on a mechanical bull. While I love the old lady, I didn't love her enough to have her come live with me again. And if she broke a hip or anything else, that's exactly what would happen.

Mom took one look at my face and knew something was wrong. "What's up? Did you find out who rented the box? Was it Trent?"

I shook my head. "It's worse. The guy said legally he can't give us a name, but he didn't think it would be a problem to give us a description. But there's a catch. Aunt Shirley has already had like three or four shots with this man and —"

"Yes," Paige said. "We've been watching."

"But that doesn't explain why you look worried," Mom said.

I took a deep breath and wished I had a drink in my hand to gulp down. "Larry said before he'd give up a description, Aunt Shirley had to ride the mechanical bull!"

Paige gasped and Mom stood up. "Over my dead body will she be riding a mechanical bull."

Relief flooded me. I knew if anyone could get us out of this situation, it was Mom.

"Get your purses," Mom said. "We're out of here."

"Wait," I said, my stomach sinking. "We can't leave without the information. I just need you to make the man tell us without Aunt Shirley getting up on the bull."

Mom didn't say anything, just marched over to Aunt Shirley. "We need to leave."

Aunt Shirley slowly turned to face Mom. "I ain't leaving until I've ridden the bull and gotten the information I came here for."

Mom and Aunt Shirley squared off. I felt my lower lip tremble as tears fill my eyes. I didn't want to see Aunt Shirley hurt, but I also didn't want to see her dragged out of here, either. Maybe getting Mom involved wasn't such a good idea.

"You're too old to ride a mechanical bull," Mom insisted.

"Please don't fight." I didn't think anyone heard me over the loud country music being played, but something must have come through, because Mom and Aunt Shirley both turned to glare at me.

After a few tense seconds, Aunt Shirley grabbed my mom by the arm and hauled us all over to an empty corner.

"I'm only going to say this one time," Aunt Shirley said. "I've lived my life on my own terms. I've done everything I ever wanted. I am an independent woman who relies on no one to do for her."

Mom opened her mouth to interrupt.

Aunt Shirley shook her head. "Not this time, Janine. This time you are going to listen to me. I grew up in the shadow of my perfect older sister, your mother. I loved her with all my heart. But it was impossible to compete with her. I was nothing like her or my parents. I learned at a very young age that I couldn't be what they

120

wanted me to be, nor did I want to be that person. That left me with the option of running. I left home and struck out on my own. On my own…meaning I've never had to answer to anyone but myself. And now that I'm older, suddenly everyone wants to treat me like I'm a child again. Telling me what's wrong with me, telling me I have to act a certain way, telling me I'm too over-the-top and I need to calm down. Well to hell with them and to hell with you."

Tears streamed down my face as I listened to Aunt Shirley give us the what-for. Mainly because it's not like we didn't deserve it. I was constantly trying to micro-manage her. Trying to control every situation we got into. I wiped my eyes and looked at Mom's rigid face. Paige grabbed my hand and squeezed.

Aunt Shirley turned to me. "I love your daughter, my great-niece. And I see a lot of her inside me, even though she rides me hard about my behavior." Aunt Shirley turned back to Mom. "But know this, Janine, never have I ever put Ryli in danger that she couldn't handle."

Hmm…well…

"And if I ever felt that we were in so much danger that we could be killed, believe me, I'd give my life to protect her. I love her like the daughter I never had. I wouldn't risk her life on a whim."

If it were possible, I think my heart broke and leaped at that admission from Aunt Shirley. I swiped at my nose with the back of my hand.

Mom looked up at the ceiling for a few seconds and then back at Aunt Shirley. "She's my only daughter, and I love her like she *is* my own. And yes, it scares me to death when you take her along on one of your wild rides." She sighed heavily. "But I know you love her and you wouldn't want anything to happen to her. So fine, I'll back off and let you two do what you do without complaint."

A grin split my face and I grabbed Mom and hugged her. Mom backing down was a huge deal. Something I didn't know she had in her to do. It was always Mom's way because she's always had to be in control. At a young age, she was both mother and father. She wasn't used to giving up the reigns.

Aunt Shirley clapped her hands. "Good. Now, let's get me on a mechanical bull so I can go back to Mystery Farms and get me a killer!"

Mom frowned. "Don't you mean get the information you need, call Sheriff Simpson, tell him what you know, and let him make an arrest?"

Aunt Shirley waved her hands in the air as she walked toward the bar. "That's what I said."

"I'm going to order another drink," Mom sighed.

Paige hugged my arm as we walked back to where Larry Tubbins sat. "That must have been cool to hear them say such nice things about you."

I smiled. "It was. Who knew Aunt Shirley felt that way?"

"Me," Paige said.

"Okay, Larry, let's get this show on the road," Aunt Shirley yelled out over the music.

Larry slammed his hands down on the bar and let out a whoop. "Right this way, Twila."

Paige snickered. "Twila? Why Twila?"

I shrugged. "I have no idea."

The four of us followed Larry over to the side of the shed where the mechanical bull was currently throwing someone off. My steps got slower the closer we got.

"What's wrong?" Paige asked.

"I don't know if I want Aunt Shirley doing this. What if she really gets hurt?"

Paige chewed her lower lip. "I know what you mean. I guess we have to trust she knows what she's doing."

I rolled my eyes at Paige. "She never knows what she's doing."

Mom, Paige, and I stood by the roped off area. My hope was bolstered a little when I realized the mats were heavily padded. Maybe when she fell it wouldn't hurt too much. Who was I kidding, this would be brutal.

Mom chuckled beside me. "I can't believe she's going to ride that bull in a dress."

I nodded. "She's going to show the world her underwear."

"That should sober everyone up fast," Paige snickered. "An old lady in granny panties."

If only Paige knew how close to the truth she was. A few months ago when Aunt Shirley and I busted a burglary ring, we ran across some red granny panties she wanted to keep for herself.

"Ladies and gentlemen," the guy running the mechanical bull controls boomed into his microphone, "let's give a warm Lazy J welcome to first-time rider, Twila Blackstone!"

The crowd clapped and whooped and whistled as Aunt Shirley took a huge bow in front of the announcer's table. Larry Tubbins was grinning like a fool.

"Twila Blackstone?" Mom asked. "Do I even want to know?"

I laughed. "I have no idea where she comes up with half the things she does."

I watched with trepidation as a studly young cowboy gently led Aunt Shirley to the bull. She was grinning and blowing kisses to the crowd. When she got to the bull, she put one foot into the strap and swung her leg over. Her dress rode up dangerously high on her thigh.

Aunt Shirley pulled her dress down as modestly as she could, then made a big show of wagging her finger at the young cowboy as though he was wanting to take a peek at her goodies.

The crowd roared with laughter. The cute cowboy played along and shrugged like he was caught red-handed. He tipped his hat to Aunt Shirley, turned to the crowd, winked, then sauntered away from the bull, leaving Aunt Shirley alone in the center of the ring.

I held my breath and waited for the bull to start moving. Aunt Shirley made a motion to the guy at the controls and he pushed a button.

The bull started off gently, only rocking back and forth a couple times. But then it suddenly shifted and dipped Aunt Shirley down and spun her around in a half circle. She was now facing us. She spied us and let out a whoop in our direction. Before I could lift my hand and wave, the bull dipped again and she spun around again. This time the rocking back and forth was faster. Aunt Shirley's white-knuckle grip on the reigns was the only sign she might not be totally in control.

"How long does she have to do this?" Paige asked shakily.

"Until she falls off or for eight seconds," I said. "At least, that's usually how it's done."

By this time, the bull was going full speed, swinging, dipping, rocking, and doing everything it could to buck Aunt Shirley off. The crowd was going wild as the fringe on Aunt Shirley's dress swung this way and that. Her tuffs of purple and white hair glittered under the neon lights.

When the buzzer finally sounded, I couldn't believe my ears…or eyes. The crazy old bat had actually stayed on the full eight seconds! The roar of the crowd was deafening as the cute cowboy came out to help Aunt Shirley down.

She grabbed hold of his hand and jumped down, then took another bow and waved before staggering out of the ring. She sauntered over to where we were standing, grinning from ear to ear.

"Told ya so!" Aunt Shirley boasted.

I gave her a hug. "That was awesome!"

Mom and Paige each congratulated Aunt Shirley on her amazing ride.

"How do you know how to ride a bull?" I asked incredulously.

Aunt Shirley smiled wistfully. "Burt Lancaster. He didn't just star in westerns, he lived them. I met him and his second wife, Norma, when I was living in LA. I learned how to ride bulls from Burt."

I lifted an eyebrow. Could some of her movie star stories really be true? I always figured she made them up to seem important. Bragging about dating Clint Eastwood, hanging with famous people. Maybe I needed to rethink my image of Aunt Shirley.

Larry stumbled over and slapped Aunt Shirley on the back. "Mighty fine riding there, little lady!"

Aunt Shirley curtsied. "I kept up my end of the bargain. Now it's your turn. Describe the person you rented the box to."

Larry Tubbins turned serious. "Well, I only remember this because it was so odd. The person opened the box under a John Smith, but the person *may* or may not have been a female."

We all collectively sucked in a breath.

"A female?" I asked. "Are you sure?"

Larry said nothing, just smirked at us.

Was it Dayna? None of this made any sense.

"Well," Aunt Shirley demanded, "what did she look like?"

Larry shrugged. "She *may* or may not have one attribute that makes her impossible to forget."

I furrowed my brow. "An attribute that's hard to forget?" I thought about the females we had as suspects. Dayna and Cybil didn't really have any outstanding features. No obvious tattoos, basic hair color, body shape. Olivia was also in that same boat. Tina, on the other hand, could stand out because of her ample cleavage, but I wasn't sure that would be enough to identify her on. So that left Bessie.

I inhaled sharply. "Could this possible female have frizzy red hair and be a little on the plump side?"

Larry just grinned.

"Bessie Terrance," the four of us said together.

CHAPTER 15

"Why?"

"This makes no sense!"

"What's the motive?"

We were all talking at once…shocked at the information we'd just received. I couldn't begin to make heads or tails from it.

We paid our bar tab and hurried out of the Lazy J Saloon toward the Falcon. Aunt Shirley and Mom were arguing over whether or not to call Sheriff Simpson with the information we'd just gathered. Mom said yes, but Aunt Shirley said she wanted to go home and think about it some more.

"That was some ride you had." We all turned and stared at Big Bad Bouncer guy.

Aunt Shirley grinned and shrugged her shoulders. "Thanks. It was nothing."

Big Bad Bouncer grunted. "How did your recon mission go? Did you get the answers you needed?"

"You bet I did," Aunt Shirley said. "Just like I said I would."

I sighed. "But now we're more confused than ever."

He nodded sagely, never once smiling. "That's how it goes sometimes. Best thing to do is study it from every angle. Don't make any rash decisions. Sometimes what's in front of you is not always what it purports to be."

I wrinkled my brow. What he said made sense. So much so, I felt like my brain was trying to tell me something. What was I missing?

It was a silent ride back to Mystery Farms. In the end, Mom agreed to go along with Aunt Shirley's request and not call Sheriff Simpson immediately. After all, it was really just circumstantial evidence. We couldn't place Bessie in the barn with the weapon. Not unless fingerprints came back from the lab with a match.

By the time we pulled into Mystery Farms, the house was shrouded in darkness. The front porch light was on, and the light in the foyer, but everything else looked dark and eerie.

Mom unlocked the front door and we quietly tiptoed up the stairs. I couldn't help but wonder where everyone else was. Did Bessie know we were on to her? Were we making a big mistake by not calling Sheriff Simson immediately? I couldn't imagine she'd run in the middle of the night, but who knew?

We whispered goodnight to Mom and Paige and then quietly made our way to our room—each of us deep in thought about what we'd discovered.

"I'm completely baffled," Aunt Shirley admitted as she shut and locked our bedroom door.

"I couldn't agree more. Of all the people it could have been, I never really saw Bessie as the killer."

Aunt Shirley wiggled out of her country dress—fringe flying everywhere. "I can't even think of a motive as to why she would blackmail the other women. Was she jealous of them?" Aunt Shirley wrinkled her nose. "Maybe she's a cougar and wanted Trent for herself."

I laughed at that thought. "That seems a little far-fetched." I pulled my pajamas out from the dresser and undressed. "Although, let's be honest, we've uncovered crazier things. How does the camcorder fit in? Obviously Trent knew about it because one of the last things he did was walk toward it to shut it off when he was with Tina."

"True."

"So did Bessie find out about Trent videotaping these women?" I asked. "Our first night together Gary Wainwright did say she was pretty tech savvy. Maybe she found out about the camcorder and somehow made photos. That's possible on those camcorders."

Aunt Shirley grabbed her silky, floor-length nightgown from the dresser. "The motive? Just to get money? Jealousy? Those are powerful reasons to kill. But I still think we are missing something."

I sighed and went into the bathroom to take off my makeup and brush my teeth. "All of that is for Sheriff Simpson to figure out. We have pretty sufficient evidence that she is the killer. How he makes it stick is on him."

Aunt Shirley leaned against the bathroom frame and watched as I finished getting ready for bed. Once I was done she reached over and snagged a container off the counter and popped her teeth out of her mouth. She looked over at my blanched face and smiled a wide gummy smile at me.

"And that's how you go to bed when you're an old woman," she gummed out.

As we snuggled down in the bed, the room pitch black, I expected to hear immediate snores. Usually it didn't take but a second for Aunt Shirley to fall asleep. Instead, she softly nudged me.

"I want to tell you something," she said. It was hard to understand her without her teeth, but I did my best to focus on what she was saying. "All those things I said about you tonight. I really meant them. I think of you as the daughter I never had. You're a smart girl with a good head on her shoulders. And you're good at solving mysteries."

I blinked back the sudden onslaught of tears that sprang to my eyes. That was probably one of the nicest things Aunt Shirley had ever said to me. Usually she just rolls her eyes and says sarcastic things to me about my life, my boyfriend, and my ability to solve a crime.

I turned on my side to face her in the dark. I tried not to laugh. She had her mouth wide open and was already snoring. So much for that bonding moment.

***

I tossed my suitcase on the bed the next morning after I'd dressed. "I'm going to go ahead and pack up some of this stuff so we don't have to spend too much time after the arrest this morning packing. Something tells me the Wainwrights aren't going to want people hanging around for very long. This is going to pretty much decimate their bed and breakfast."

Aunt Shirley poked her head out of the bathroom. "Sounds good. After I finish putting on my face, I'll do the same."

"What time are you calling Sheriff Simpson?" I asked.

"Right before we go down for breakfast. I'm still not convinced we haven't missed something, but we do need to at least get Bessie brought in for questioning. I did some thinking during the night last night. Your snoring kept me up."

I rolled my eyes. I don't snore. She probably just had heartburn from all the drinking she'd done and didn't want to admit it.

Aunt Shirley came out of the bathroom carrying her gigantic makeup bag. "I guess with the knowledge that she opened the P.O. Box, and the added bonus of Bessie knowing her way around a computer so she could just send herself the pictures from the camcorder, it's pretty open and shut."

I smiled. "You're just upset because there's not a Columbo-like finish. Bessie hasn't confessed and said why she did it. Admit it, you like that ribbon on the package."

Aunt Shirley scowled at me. "I suppose I'm upset that we won't be around to hear the rest of the story."

I closed my suitcase and picked up my cell phone. Aunt Shirley grabbed her oversized pink purse and cell phone.

"Why're you taking your purse?" I asked.

Aunt Shirley smiled secretly. "Because you never know when something might come in handy."

I groaned. "You *want* a crazy confession from Bessie, don't you? You want some excuse to reach inside your purse and get out—what? Did you bring your nunchucks again?" I sucked in a breath. "Please tell me you didn't bring your nunchucks!"

Aunt Shirley waved her hand in irritation. "No, I didn't bring the nunchucks. And just because I believe in being prepared doesn't mean I *want* something to happen. It means I'm the smart one in the group."

I narrowed my eyes at her. "You know something, don't you?"

Aunt Shirley shook her head. "No. Not for sure. But I have been tossing a couple things around. I think it will be good for Bessie to go to the station. This way the others will let their guard down."

I knew better than to ask more questions, so I leaned quietly against the wall as Aunt Shirley dialed Sheriff Simpson's number. I could tell from the one-sided conversation he was just as surprised as we were at the discovery.

"He said he'll be here in about half an hour."

I pushed off the wall. "Then let's go bring down a killer."

CHAPTER 16

As I knocked on Mom's bedroom door to let them know we were ready, Olivia Banner and her husband closed the door to their room.

"I don't know about you," Olivia said with a smile, "but I can't wait to leave today. Do you think Sheriff Simpson will be by today with an arrest?"

I blinked in surprise at her. It was almost like she was a fly on our wall. "I'm sure he knows something by now. Hopefully he'll be able to take someone in for further questioning."

They moved past us and continued down the stairs. "See you in the parlor," Olivia called back.

"That was creepy," Aunt Shirley said.

I nodded. "But maybe they're just excited to get back to their house and make a fresh start. I do like knowing that something good has come out of this terrible tragedy."

Mom threw open the door. "Paige is about ready. She had a pretty rough morning. She insists she wants to try and come down for breakfast, but then I want her to come back up here and lie down for a little bit before we head home."

"That's fine," I said. "Aunt Shirley and I pretty much have our stuff packed and ready to go anyway."

Paige shuffled to the door. "I'm sorry about this. I really thought by now the morning sickness would have faded."

Mom wrapped her arms around Paige. "Don't you worry. I'm sure Aunt Shirley and Ryli can find something to do this morning while you nap after breakfast."

Paige laughed self-consciously. "I suppose I should be grateful for all the naps I can get in now. Because something tells me when this baby comes, there'll be no rest for me."

The parlor was already in full swing. Olivia and Brian were sitting on the couch talking with Wayne Skaggs. Wayne was wearing another suit and tie, this time with an orange handkerchief.

The Wainwrights were passing out coffee and laughing with Olivia and Brian. Tina was sitting by the fireplace watching Dayna pour her a mimosa. Stewart was scowling in the corner, but at least the phone was out of his hand. He waved off a drink when Dayna asked if he wanted anything.

"Right on time," Gary Wainwright called out as we walked into the parlor. "Coffee, tea, or mimosa this morning?"

Paige asked for peppermint tea to help settle her stomach, while Mom and I asked for coffee.

"For you Aunt Shirley?" Gary asked.

"Coffee."

I did a double take. Aunt Shirley passed on a mimosa? Was she coming down with something? Was the world coming to an end? Was she finally growing up?

"I'll save the mimosa for breakfast," she added.

And there it was. The proof that all was still right in the world.

"Breakfast is ready to be served," Bessie said from the doorway.

I had to admit, she didn't look like someone who'd taken a hammer to someone's head less than twenty-four hours ago. But then again, I'd been wrong about people so many times it wasn't even funny.

We all followed Bessie into the dining room. This morning she had breakfast set up buffet style. We lined up as Dayna took our drink orders, and Bessie stood behind the food-ladened table to help serve.

Luckily I was sitting at the table facing a window that overlooked the driveway, so I saw Sheriff Simpson's patrol car bumping down the long driveway before the others had a chance to see. I shoved the last of my eggs and bacon in before taking a drink of my coffee. It was time for the show to start.

The ringing of the doorbell had everyone else going quiet. A silent look passed between Gary and Cybil Wainwright as they went to go answer the door.

I looked surreptitiously at Aunt Shirley. She'd just finished off her mimosa and looked quite pleased with herself.

No one said a word as Sheriff Simpson took off his hat and walked in behind the Wainwrights. Gary and Cybil went back to their chairs and sat down.

"There's been some new development in the case," Sheriff Simpson began. "I want it known that I'm not here to officially arrest anyone yet, but I do have enough evidence to take someone in for further questioning down at the station. I'm also going to request consent to search their bedroom."

I looked around the table. Everyone looked scared and no one met the Sheriff's eye. If I didn't know better, I'd say every person at the table expected to be taken down to the station and questioned further. I guess Aunt Shirley was right...we were missing something.

Sheriff Simpson shoved his hat back on his head and took out his handcuffs. "Bessie Terrance, I'm going to ask you to place your hands behind your back. Again, you are not under arrest, this is just for safety precautions."

Bessie looked like she'd been slapped. Her mouth dropped open and her cheeks and neck matched the red of her hair. "Me? I haven't done anything! I didn't kill Trent!"

Bessie looked wildly around the room. I didn't know if she was looking for an escape route or for someone to tell her it was just a misunderstanding. Sheriff Simpson gently turned her around and put the handcuffs on her. Bessie started to cry.

"Do you give me consent to go through your room and the kitchen?" Sheriff Simpson asked.

"Of course! You won't find anything because there's nothing for you to find!"

"Thank you." He leaned over and clicked the radio mic on his shoulder. "Permission given to search suspect's room and kitchen." He gently turned Bessie around to face him. "You and I will now go down to the station for further questioning."

"Mr. Wainwright!" Bessie cried. "I haven't done anything! I swear!"

Gary Wainwright stood up. "Is it okay if I come down to the station to give her a ride home, Sheriff?"

Sheriff Simpson nodded. "That will be fine, Gary."

I could hear voices in the foyer and footsteps on the stairs. The other deputies weren't wasting any time on searching Bessie's room and the kitchen. Sheriff Simpson led a weeping Bessie from the room.

No one spoke for a full ten seconds, then chaos erupted. I didn't say anything, just finished off the last of my coffee. Once the conversation died down, everyone seemed antsy and anxious to get to their room.

"We will be leaving immediately," Stewart announced as he pushed his chair back from the table. "Tina, let's go."

Tina kept her head down and followed her husband out of the room. Olivia and Brian were next to escape.

"Aunt Shirley," Gary Wainwright said. "Can I speak to you for a moment?"

Aunt Shirley and Gary left the room, and Mom, Paige, and I offered to help Dayna and Cybil clean the dishes, but they wouldn't hear of it, especially since it was obvious no one would be getting into the kitchen anytime soon. They both shooed us out of the room.

"Now what?" Mom asked as we stood in the empty foyer. "Do we get our stuff and leave immediately or…"

Aunt Shirley walked in and shook her head. "No. We need to stay on for a little while longer."

Mom closed her eyes. "Please don't get held hostage or get kidnapped or anything else today."

Aunt Shirley grinned. "No promises, Janine. But I'll try not to."

Wayne Skaggs strolled into the foyer from the dining room. "I'm going to change clothes and then head out to take care of the horses for Gary while he's gone. It shouldn't take me more than an hour and a half. Janine, when I return, maybe you and I can go for a walk before you leave?"

I saw the look of panic in Mom's eyes. Before anyone could say anything, Paige moaned. "I'm really not feeling well. Morning sickness, you know. Janine, could you help me up to our room?"

Nice move! Blame it on the baby!

I hid my smile as Mom nodded her head. "Of course. I'm sorry, Wayne. I think I'm going to have to take a raincheck. Maybe another time."

Wayne nodded his head stiffly and watched Mom and Paige climb the stairs. "Well, ladies, you two stay out of trouble now, you hear." He sauntered up the stairs and turned right at the top to enter the west wing.

"Let's go upstairs until the deputies leave," Aunt Shirley said.

We met Tina and Stewart dragging suitcases behind them in the hallway as we unlocked our door.

"Are you guys leaving now?" Aunt Shirley asked.

"Yes," Stewart said gruffly. "We are not staying in this crazy place one more minute."

I looked at Tina. Her eyes were red from crying, and she wouldn't look me in the eye. I couldn't help but feel a little sorry for her. It was obvious her only crime was needing attention. Even after all this hoopla, her husband still wasn't going to give her what she needed.

"Good luck," I whispered to her.

She gave me a weak smile and meekly followed her husband down the hall. Aunt Shirley unlocked our door and threw her purse on the bed.

"Before he left, Gary Wainwright gave me the master key set. I can now get into any room I want."

I shook my head as though to clear it. "Wait. What?"

Aunt Shirley grinned. "You heard right. That's what he wanted to see me about. He opened this box behind the desk in the foyer and gave me the master keys. He wants us to do whatever we can to find the murderer. I guess he doesn't believe Bessie would do this."

I narrowed my eyes at her. "You know which room you want to search, don't you?"

"Yep. I have a hunch. I'm still not sure how it all plays out, but I like this scenario better than anything else we've thought of with Bessie as the killer."

"Who?"

Aunt Shirley just smiled and shook her head. "I'll tell you when the time's right. I want to lay down for about twenty minutes and think. The deputies should be gone by then and we can make our move."

I blew out a sigh. I knew better than to probe her when she needed to think. I got out my cell phone and sent Garrett a text letting him know Sheriff Simpson took our cook, Bessie, in for further questioning and that we should be cleared to leave shortly. I purposely left out the fact that Aunt Shirley did not think Bessie was the killer because I didn't want him to worry.

A few minutes later I received a text back saying for me to drive safe on the way home and to let him know when we would be leaving.

I hated only telling him half the truth, but by now I've come to learn that Garrett will never trust that Aunt Shirley and I can handle ourselves.

I'd just set my phone down and closed my eyes when Aunt Shirley's phone alarm went off.

"Let's go." She picked up her massive purse and slung it over her shoulder. "They should be gone by now."

I silently followed her out of the room. We stopped at the top of the stairs and looked outside. The two patrol cars were just pulling out.

"Perfect timing," Aunt Shirley cackled. "Let's roll!"

CHAPTER 17

I silently followed her into the west wing until we came to Wayne's bedroom door. Aunt Shirley took out the master key and pushed open the door. She put her finger to her lips to signal me to be quiet.

I silently shut the door behind me as we stood in the center of Wayne's room and looked around. It was laid out like the others. He had a bed, a desk, a dresser, and a bathroom.

"I'm going to look through his desk drawers," Aunt Shirley whispered. "You look through the dresser."

I had no idea what I was looking for, but I did as she requested. I opened the top drawer and found nothing out of the ordinary. In fact, I found nothing strange as I went through all the drawers.

"I thought so," Aunt Shirley murmured.

"What did you find?"

Aunt Shirley held up a collage of pictures. Some of Wayne in costume, others with him and another woman and a child. I peered down and sucked in my breath. "Is that Trent? Omigosh! Did he kill his own son or something?"

That thought nearly knocked me over, and I plopped down on the edge of Wayne's bed. I couldn't believe he'd be heartless enough to kill his own son. I dropped my hands and head between my legs and closed my eyes.

"I don't think it's his son. Maybe nephew or step-son."

I didn't care how she spun the tale, I was about to throw up at the thought. I opened my eyes and something colorful caught my eye. I started to pull on the strand and realized it was stuck because I was sitting on it. I stood up off the bed and reached down to pull the strand the rest of the way out.

"Look what I found," I whispered and held up a frizzy red wig.

Aunt Shirley looked over at me. "That's exactly what I was looking for. The whole female thing threw me off. But last night when I couldn't sleep, I started thinking about everything that had gone on while we were here. And I remembered how good Wayne was at disguises. Put on a frizzy red wig, sunglasses, add some girth to him like he did with the Colonel Musgaard character, throw on a dress, and he could pull it off." She picked up a small recorder inside the desk and pushed play. The sounds of an electric typewriter filled the silent bedroom. "And that's how he got around the timeline."

"What do you mean?" I asked.

"Yes," an angry voice said from the doorway. "Whatever do you mean?"

I turned around and saw Wayne Skaggs with his arms outstretched…holding a snub-nosed .38 revolver.

Pointed directly at my chest, I might add.

Wayne straightened from the doorframe and shut the door behind him. "I figured you'd take the bait I laid out for you. I tell you I'll be out of my room for an hour or so and look who shows up."

He stopped two feet in front of me. "You don't want to make a sound," he told Aunt Shirley. "I have no problem capping her right here."

Aunt Shirley's face turned ashen. "I understand."

He motioned for Aunt Shirley to join me near the bed. She picked up her purse and walked slowly toward me. I could see the wheels turning in her head.

Wayne reached into the bottom drawer of his desk and pulled out two huge zip ties. My heart lurched at the thought of what he intended to do to us.

I sat down on the edge of the bed and watched as Aunt Shirley made a fuss over situating herself just right as she sat down on the edge of the bed next to me. She plopped her oversize purse down on her lap, fisted both of her hands side-by-side, and rested them on top of her purse. I knew Aunt Shirley well enough to know that every gesture or word she said from here on out would have a purpose.

"Can you at least tell us why and how?" Aunt Shirley asked as Wayne slipped a zip tie over my wrists and pulled tightly.

"Ow!" I couldn't help the cry. I wasn't expecting that kind of pain.

"Shut up!" Wayne hissed.

He didn't say anything as he moved down to where Aunt Shirley was calmly sitting. He slipped the zip tie over her side-by-side wrists and pulled tight. She grunted in pain. White hot rage filled my body, and at that moment I wanted nothing more than to pull off Wayne Skaggs' arms and beat him to death with his own limbs.

"This was really a simple plan," Wayne said once the zip ties were in place. "I came here first over a year ago, then realized what a gold mine I was sitting on. I knew I'd need help executing my plan, so I brought my sister's boy in on the scam. He only had one part he needed to play, but he couldn't even do that right!"

The more Wayne talked the more his face contorted with rage. He tucked the gun into his waistband and then threw an empty suitcase on the bed behind me. He grabbed and shoved whatever he could lay his hands on into the suitcase.

"Trent's only part he needed to play," Aunt Shirley said, "was to pretend to fall in love with Dayna, right?"

Wayne grunted. "But the kid couldn't keep it in his pants enough to even do that." He straightened and drew in a deep breath. "Seeing as how I love a good story, I'll tell you the rest before I kill you."

His matter-of-fact statement had me nearly peeing my pants. How would he kill us without everyone hearing? How much longer before people started looking for us? Who was still here? Cybil and Dayna. Mom and Paige. Maybe Olivia and Brian.

"The minute I stepped foot on Mystery Farms, I knew I deserved this place. I bid my time, getting to know the Wainwrights, finding their weakness." A wicked smile twisted his face. "Their weakness is their niece. So after a couple months of being here, I convinced Gary he needed to hire someone to take care of the horses and help out around the farm more—take some of that pressure off of him, this way he could focus on the business more. He agreed and put an ad out in the paper. I wrote to Trent and told him the plan. He wasn't allowed to tell anyone he knew me. He was just supposed to say he knew horses, give some backstory about living in Wyoming on a horse ranch, and then come here and woo the niece. I'd take care of everything after that."

I swallowed hard. "How would you take care of it?"

Wayne shook himself as though coming back to reality. He looked over at me and scowled. "After Trent married the little brat, her uncle was gonna have a little accident. Cybil would be so distraught over the death of her husband, she'd pretty much hand over the farm to me—or Trent. Either way I was the winner."

"But Trent didn't keep up his end of the agreement, did he?" Aunt Shirley asked.

Wayne let out a growl and slammed the suitcase shut. I jumped nearly a foot in the air. "No, he didn't. One day I came across him watching a video he'd taken of him and another woman. I waited until he left his office and found the camcorder. I realized then I could probably make some quick cash until I could talk the idiot into getting on board with my plan. He had no idea I would sneak into his office and get photos to blackmail those women."

Wayne crossed in front of me and grabbed the recorder off his desk. "Using Bessie as the fall person was really just a stroke of genius. I came across the wig one day in my trunk of tricks, and it just clicked." He pushed play on his recorder and the sound of typing filled the air. His lips twisted. "She deserved it! She came over here banging on the door one too many times. Demanding I stop writing. Demanding I get a computer like everyone else and write silently. Demanding, demanding, demanding." He suddenly threw the recorder across the room. It hit the wall and shattered into pieces. I let out a little yelp. "But over the years I've come to learn that people see what they want to see. I go into the post office and open a box looking like a female—frizzy red hair, plump in all the right places, conservative dress—people expect me to be a female. They aren't going to question it too much."

Wayne looked at me as if seeing me for the first time. His pupils dilated and I nearly fainted in fright. He reached over and grabbed one of his silk handkerchiefs off the top of the dresser and stuffed it in my mouth. Panic flooded my body. I knew it was only a matter of minutes before he killed us both.

Inches from my face, Wayne reached behind him and pulled out his gun. "What I hadn't anticipated," he thumped the gun against my temple to emphasize his words, "was you two meddling twits." He stood up and stared menacingly down at us. "I figured just the normal wanna-be crime solvers would come this weekend. I knew it was my lucky day when I saw on the reservation board that two of Trent's former flings would be here. It was the perfect time to set Trent up. The Wainwrights would confront him with the pictures, setting themselves up as potential murderers. Then there was Dayna, the jealous ex, two old flings who were being blackmailed..." He leaned back down to scowl in my face. "Everything should have been *perfect*!" Spittle flew from his mouth and hit my cheek.

For the record, gagging with a handkerchief stuffed in your mouth is very difficult to do.

Wayne stood up suddenly and shifted gears once again. The guy was definitely off his rocker. He shoved a handkerchief into Aunt Shirley's mouth then stood and looked at us. "So now I have to leave *my* home. The very place that should have been mine, just because you two couldn't leave well enough alone!" I barely resisted the urge to duck as more spittle flew out of his mouth. "I know I can't shoot you and risk bringing everyone running. Lucky for you I got just the thing. A bit of rope to strangle the life right out of you."

He laughed manically and went into the bathroom. I looked wide-eyed at Aunt Shirley. She shook her head at me then closed her eyes. I could hear Wayne cursing and shoving things around in the bathroom. He obviously couldn't find the rope. Thank God!

Aunt Shirley coughed slightly and I turned to look at her. I could tell she was trying to grin but couldn't with the handkerchief stuffed in her mouth. She brought her bound hands up, twisted her wrists until they went from being side-by-side to facing each other, then quickly wriggled out of the zip ties.

I couldn't believe how quick she'd been! I tried doing the same, but my wrists were already facing each other. Obviously I didn't know the right way to get tied up with zip ties.

She shook her head at me and yanked the handkerchief quickly out of her mouth. Unfortunately, her top dentures were still attached to the handkerchief and they flew across the room, hit the wall, and fell to the floor. I was so shocked I couldn't help but giggle.

"Found it!" Wayne cried triumphantly from the bathroom.

I could feel my body going into panic mode. Not only were my teeth starting to chatter around the gag, but my body couldn't stop shaking.

Aunt Shirley picked up her purse and quickly unzipped it. She reached in and pulled out a handful of silver circles. The minute Wayne rounded the corner out of the bathroom, Aunt Shirley started throwing!

Two of them struck Wayne in the chest and one in the face. He brought his hands up to deflect the blows, but it was no use. Aunt Shirley was throwing the discs with all her might. It wasn't until she reached in her purse for more that I realized they were ninja stars!

I laughed hysterically at the thought of toothless Aunt Shirley hurling ninja stars at a murderer. Wayne let out a bellow of rage and opened the door at his back. Aunt Shirley didn't let up. She grabbed her purse with her left hand and kept on throwing with her right.

I jumped up off the bed, wrists still tied and mouth still gagged, bent down and picked up Aunt Shirley's false teeth as fast as I could with confined hands, and followed them down the hallway. No way was I missing out on this!

I could hear Wayne's screams of rage and pain. Aunt Shirley was gaining on him and I'd bet anything those stars were taking their toll on poor Wayne.

I spotted Wayne and Aunt Shirley at the top of the staircase. Wayne pivoted and turned to face Aunt Shirley. He whipped out the gun from his waistband and aimed it at Aunt Shirley. I let out a blood curdling scream—well, as much as I could with the handkerchief still shoved in my mouth. At the same time Wayne fired the gun, Aunt Shirley swung her oversized purse and hit Wayne on the side of his head. The force knocked him off his feet and he fell down…down the flight of stairs. His screams echoed in my head.

I suddenly realized it wasn't just Wayne's screams that echoed in my head, but my own screams as well. And Aunt Shirley's? What was going on? Why was everyone rushing toward me screaming? Mom, Paige, Aunt Shirley? And why did my arm feel like it was on fire?

At least there was good news…I couldn't feel myself clutching Aunt Shirley's false teeth anymore.

CHAPTER 18

You can't even begin to imagine how much begging and pleading I had to do for Garrett not to haul butt down to the hospital I had to be checked into. I tried bribing the EMTs to say I was okay, but they didn't bite.

Wayne's bullet did make a connection—into my arm. Well, not exactly into it, really more of a graze. And that's what I had to keep repeating to Garrett. It wasn't like I was actually shot, just more grazed. But Garrett knew enough to know what that meant.

The truth was, it felt like I'd been shot. The pain was so intense I thought I would explode. But I knew for the sake of my family that I could never let on how much it actually hurt.

When Mom first reached my side, she was an absolute mess, yelling at me and Aunt Shirley about once again getting in over our heads. She was so mad she said words I didn't know she knew. Then she switched gears and started crying and kissing me…but still giving Aunt Shirley the evil eye.

Paige was crying and wailing, then trying to say some of it was hormones from the baby. But I didn't believe it for a minute. I knew from their reaction that I needed to suck it up and live with it. Otherwise, I'd never hear the end of it on how I almost went and got myself killed…again!

I especially needed to get over it where Aunt Shirley was concerned. Aunt Shirley had been deathly quiet the whole time I was being worked on. Mom's yelling, Paige's crying, I expected that. But Aunt Shirley hadn't said a word the whole time they patched me up. And that scared me to death. I knew she was terrified.

So by the time I got to the hospital, I knew I had to pretend I was fine, and that I needed to convince everyone that it really didn't hurt very much. I even succeeded in convincing Garrett not to come down and arrest Aunt Shirley for whatever accusation it was he made up on the spot. And when Hank called the hospital to check in on me, I promised to give him an exclusive once again...even go into detail about how I'd been shot.

I held in all the emotion I was feeling and only let it out when I was alone.

The truth is, I was scared to death when I finally realized I'd been shot. The adrenaline I'd been running on came to a crashing halt when the reality of what'd happened finally broke through.

But the good news is, I only had to stay one night in the hospital. Mom stayed with me while Aunt Shirley and Paige went back to Mystery Farms. Sheriff Simpson and his deputies wasted no time in arresting Wayne—who also suffered injuries. He had two broken legs and a broken arm. Couldn't have happened to a better person if you ask me.

Monday morning the doctor came around, gave me a prescription for pain medication, and released me back into the care of my mother. By ten o'clock we were on the road back to Granville. I jokingly asked Mom if we could hit some wineries on the way home since we hadn't done any wine tasting yet. That earned me a glare.

Luckily, I slept most of the way home, thanks to the yummy pain killers the doctor gave me.

"Wake up, sleepy head," Garrett crooned in my ear.

I smile and rubbed my chin against the side of his neck. "I don't want to. I want to stay right here, just like this."

Garrett chuckled. "Ryli, we are still inside the car. We should at least get out."

I opened my eyes and kissed him. I put everything I had into it. I blocked out the pain, the fear, everything…and just kissed him like I never wanted to let him go. Which I didn't.

Garrett finally broke off the kiss. "I missed you. And I can't believe you went and got yourself shot."

I laughed and slowly opened my eyes. "How big of a lecture am I going to get?"

"Huge! Maybe not quite as big as the lecture Aunt Shirley is going to get."

I laid my hand on his arm. "Please don't. You want to yell at me, sigh, shake your head…that's fine. I can handle it. But please don't make Aunt Shirley feel worse than she already does. It was a great weekend, and I just want to remember it that way."

I could see Garrett was wrestling with my request. He wanted nothing more than to do the man/cop thing and lecture and remind Aunt Shirley and me of how silly we were, and we weren't real investigators, and how he always knew something like this would finally happen. It was the same lecture he gave every time we got into a mess like this.

Only this time I wasn't sure if Aunt Shirley could take it. On the drive home, as she sat in the backseat of the Falcon with me, every time I opened my eyes she was there giving me pats and smiles. But I could see the worry in her face.

"Fine," Garrett growled and kissed me again. "You have one free pass this time."

"So you admit there will probably be a next time, right?" I joked.

"Please don't make me throttle you on your first night back."

I grinned and pulled him in for another kiss. I was obviously kissed deprived.

***

It took about a week for me to recover and go back to work. Hank got his exclusive for the paper, even though he was quite pissy with me for taking another week off for an "extended vacation" as he so eloquently put my recovery time.

I tried to get Aunt Shirley to stay with me while I recovered, but she begged off saying I needed my rest. I didn't like how far apart we seemed to have grown since my accident. I knew I'd have to put my foot down and demand we talk about the elephant in the room soon.

Mom decided to celebrate my introduction back into society with a dinner at her house. I called Aunt Shirley to tell her I'd come by and pick her up, but she said Garrett already made arrangements to pick her up after he collected me. I wasn't quite sure what to make of that. Usually Garrett had to be bribed to pick up Aunt Shirley.

When we pulled into the circle drive at the Manor, Aunt Shirley was already standing outside waiting for us. She got in Garrett's truck with no fuss or mouthiness. So unlike Aunt Shirley. We drove in silence to Mom's.

"What's going on?" I asked Aunt Shirley as we pulled into Mom's driveway and parked behind Paige and Matt's car. Garrett shut off the engine.

Aunt Shirley shook her head. "Nothing."

I twisted around to look at her, and only winced once. I still didn't have full use of my arm, and certain movements were still painful. "You've been silent since we returned from our trip. Now tell me what's going on."

Aunt Shirley looked at Garrett then back at me. Her eyes filled with tears. "Oh, Ryli."

My heart seized. "What? What is it? Are you dying?"

Aunt Shirley laughed. "No, I'm not dying, you ninny! I'm just…" She sighed and look out the window.

I knew that look. That was the look of Aunt Shirley not talking. And when Aunt Shirley didn't want to talk—nothing could make her talk.

Mom stuck her head out the front door. "Everything okay?"

Garrett stuck his head out the window. "Everything's fine. Ryli and Aunt Shirley are just talking."

Mom walked down the front steps and opened the back door. "What's going on?" Mom asked as she slid inside and shut the door. "Why aren't you guys coming inside?"

I shrugged. "I told Aunt Shirley I want to throw this out on the table. I want her to tell me what's wrong."

"Aunt Shirley," Mom said. "Is there something wrong? Are you okay?"

After a few seconds Aunt Shirley spoke. "I'm just real sorry how things turned out, Ryli. I never meant for you to get hurt. For you to get shot."

154

I jerked back. "I know that, Aunt Shirley. Why would you think I wouldn't know that?"

Aunt Shirley leaned forward on the seat and reached over to clasp my hand. "I wasn't kidding when I said you were the daughter I never had. I love you so much. And then I went and promised your mother I'd protect you with my life, and I failed."

"You didn't fail," I whispered over the lump that suddenly formed in my throat. "If anyone is at fault, it's me. I should have just let you get the guy. Instead, I jumped up, still tied up, and went running after you. Not to save you, but to see what you'd do to him once you got him! If I'd have been thinking, I'd have stayed put and waited for you to come back and get me. So you see, you didn't fail me, Aunt Shirley."

Aunt Shirley nodded. "Yes, I did. I went full steam after a man who had not only tied us up, but had a gun pulled on us. I went after him without a care in the world—mainly because it's how I've always lived. I've only had myself to look after. But now it's different, and as much as I love going on these adventures with you, I can't help but think I'm putting you in harm's way too much."

I sucked in my breath. I didn't like where this was going at all.

Aunt Shirley sat back in her seat. She looked defeated and sad. "I really think it's too dangerous. I think maybe we need to take some time from each other."

My mouth dropped open. I saw Garrett nod his head, and that made me angry. "No! Absolutely not!"

"Now, Ryli," Garrett started in, "what your aunt says is—"

"The biggest load of horse poop I ever heard!" I exclaimed. "I'm not letting you take the brunt of what happened, Aunt Shirley. I was just as culpable as you. And you aren't the only one that gets something from our relationship. As much as I roll my eyes and say you are a pain in my butt, I really don't mean it. I look forward to seeing you every day. I look forward to whatever stupid adventure you're going to get us dragged into. Before you came around, my life was boring. I had a boring job. I never did anything crazy." I swiped at the tears falling from my eyes. "I can't imagine not having you around, not having someone dragging me kicking and screaming into impossible situations. So, no. You aren't going to take the blame for what happened to me and my arm. And you aren't going to keep your distance from me. I won't allow it."

I heard Garrett sigh and nearly laughed. Poor guy had no idea when he pursued a relationship with me how hard it would actually be.

"Ryli's right," Mom said. "As much as it pains me to say this, because I realize I'm all but giving you permission to be reckless, but I feel Ryli has grown a lot in the six months you guys have gotten close. Before the first murder in October, you two would see each other once a week or so, and then go about your own business. Now there is a true connection. A true family connection. And as much as it hurts to think of the things you two do together, I can't help but see how important it is in your relationship. So as much as I wanted to blame Aunt Shirley for what happened to you, Ryli. I know I can't."

Aunt Shirley chuckled. "You were pretty pissed at me the day they wheeled her in the ambulance after she was shot."

Mom's lips twitched. "I *was* pissed at you. I was so mad I wanted to take one of those ninja stars you were scrambling around trying to pick up and throw one at you!"

Garrett inhaled sharply. "You have throwing stars? That's how you took the guy down? With *throwing* stars?"

I couldn't help but laugh. "You should have seen her. She was whipping them so fast out of her purse and chucking them at Wayne. He was screaming and trying to dodge them as he ran. It was the funniest thing I'd seen in a long time."

Aunt Shirley chuckled. "It *was* pretty comical. Especially when you consider I was yelling at him with no teeth in!"

"What happened to your teeth?" Garrett asked. "Wait, no. Don't tell me. I still want to eat tonight."

Mom, Aunt Shirley, and I laughed heartily at Garrett's face. It felt good to finally release the breath we all seemed to have been holding since the incident. I didn't think my heart could feel any fuller than it did right now.

Doc came outside the house and hollered out to us. "Everything okay out here?"

Mom opened her door and slid out. "Come inside soon. We are ready to eat when you are."

I watched as Mom and Doc walked hand in hand back inside. "You know," I mused. "I really think something serious is about to happen with those two."

Garrett smiled. "Is that so?"

I nodded. "Yep. I just have this weird feeling about tonight."

"Oh, you do, huh?" Garrett leaned over and kissed my nose. "You're really something, Ryli Jo Sinclair, you know that?"

I preened at his praise. "I know." I turned back to Aunt Shirley. "So are we good?"

She grinned at me. "We're good. Let's go inside. I could use a drink after all this touchy-feeling crap."

Garrett took my good hand in his and we walked toward the front door. "I'm not so sure I'm good with this decision you and Aunt Shirley have made."

I grinned and kissed him. "Yes, you are."

He grunted.

A car door slammed and Hank and Mindy walked toward us. "I didn't know you guys were coming," I said as I hugged Mindy.

Mindy smiled at Garrett. "We wouldn't miss this for the world."

I gave Paige a big hug when I saw her. It'd been a few days since I last saw her, and I swear she looked even bigger. Of course, I wasn't going to be stupid enough to tell her that. We all took turns congratulating Paige and rubbing her belly. She took the ribbing good-naturedly, although I saw her cower in fear when Aunt Shirley squatted down and told the baby all the things she was going to teach her.

Dinner was a delicious meal of salad, grilled veggies, and salmon. Even though the outdoor table sat eight, Mom found a way for the nine of us to squeeze in and still be comfortable. The cool, spring air was just what we all needed to forget about the life and death situation we'd recently been in.

For dessert Doc had made a strawberry poke cake. Just so he wouldn't wonder if it was any good, I forced myself to have two pieces. I finished off my glass of pinot noir, which I could finally have now that the pain pills were gone, when Garrett stood up from the table.

Every eye turned to him. I looked around the table and realized I was the only person surprised when he stood and held up his hand. "Most of you know the true reason why you were invited here tonight." He turned to me and drew me from my chair so we stood and faced each other. My heart started to beat out of my chest.

"Ryli, I've enjoyed these last six months. And even though I fought this pull for so long because of our age difference, I've come to realize that it's ridiculous for me to make that be our biggest obstacle. I just wasn't prepared for you. I was used to living alone, being alone. I had the military, and then I had my job. I thought those things were enough for me, but I was wrong." He grabbed hold of my hands. "Ryli, I love the intelligent woman you are, the fierce independence you seem to have." He blew out a sigh and looked at Aunt Shirley. "And, yes, I've also come to love the quirky, silly things you do that leave my heart in my stomach."

I grinned at that statement. And because I knew in my heart where this speech was going, I wanted to yank my hand out of his grasp and wipe it on my pants…but I refrained. Wine made me retain water, and I may need that extra bit of hand sweat to help slide the ring on.

Garrett reached out and took a box from Matt. I made eye contact with Paige. She was squirming and doing a victory dance in her chair.

"Ryli, I want to spend the rest of my life with you. To grow old with you, to one day start a family with you. Whatever we decided, I want it to be together." Garrett opened the box to reveal the ring to me. I could hardly speak. I suddenly wished I'd been lifting weights like I kept telling myself I would do. The ring looked like it weighed a good five pounds!

"Ryli Jo Sinclair, will you marry me?"

I felt myself nod as tears ran down my face. Garrett lifted the ring out of the box and slid it up my finger. It was a perfect fit. I squealed and threw my arms around him. He hugged me back, laughing. And then we kissed.

After a few minutes, I heard Hank and Aunt Shirley grumble good-naturedly, and I knew I needed to break apart from Garrett and show my ring off.

"Let's see it," Aunt Shirley demanded.

I turned to see Mom, Paige, Mindy, and Aunt Shirley all huddled around waiting to get a look at my ring finger. Garrett was receiving handshakes and back slaps from the guys. Hank handed him a glass of bourbon and told him he might as well get used to needing a glass of this every night if he was going to be calling me wife. I grinned like an idiot at that statement.

"First thing we need to do is find a wedding dress," Mom said.

I groaned. "How about I just be engaged for a while."

"I hear that new quilt and fabric shop has some beautiful tulle," Paige said as though I hadn't spoken.

"Oh, a handmade veil," Aunt Shirley gasped. "I think that would be perfect!"

I rolled my eyes at Garrett. Although inside I was secretly enjoying the pampering. It looked like things were finally going my way.

A half an hour later when everyone was gone, I walked a tipsy Aunt Shirley out to Garrett's car. We'd opened a couple bottles of champagne to celebrate, and Aunt Shirley celebrated just a little too much.

"I've been thinkin'," Aunt Shirley slurred slightly. "We should take some self-defensen classes you and me." She flipped her hand back and forth between us about seven times. "You and me. We may need to learn to defend ourselves a little more. Whaddaya think?"

I laughed and put her in the back seat. "Self-defensen classes, huh?"

Aunt Shirley nodded. "Yep."

"Why not? What harm can come from learning some self-defense moves?"

Me and my big mouth.

****

Ready for Book 5 in the Ryli Sinclair Mystery series, Veiled in Murder? Just click here https://www.amazon.com/gp/product/B07FZSS6Q6?ref_=dbs_pwh_calw_4&storeType=ebooks !! Happy reading!

About the Author

Jenna writes in the genres of cozy/paranormal cozy/romantic comedy. Her humorous characters and stories revolve around over-the-top family members, creative murders, and there's always a positive element of the military in her stories. Jenna currently lives in Missouri with her fiancé, step-daughter, Nova Scotia duck tolling retriever dog, Brownie, and her tuxedo-cat, Whiskey. She is a former court reporter turned educator turned full-time writer. She has a Master's degree in Special Education, and an Education Specialist degree in Curriculum and Instruction. She also spent twelve years in full-time ministry.

When she's not writing, Jenna likes to attend beer and wine tastings, go antiquing, visit craft festivals, and spend time with her family and friends. You can friend request her on Facebook under Jenna St. James, and don't forget to visit her website at http://jennastjames.com. Be sure to sign up for her newsletter so you can hear about latest releases.